THE PAWPRINT ADVENTURES
THE YOUNG ADULT NOVELS
OF L. FRANK BAUM

SAM STEELE'S ADVENTURES

THE AMAZING
BUBBLE CAR

"The Escape!"

SAM STEELE'S ADVENTURES

THE AMAZING BUBBLE CAR

BY L. FRANK BAUM
Author of the Oz Books

Illustrated by Howard Heath

THE PAWPRINT ADVENTURES
HUNGRY TIGER PRESS

SAM STEELE'S ADVENTURES
THE AMAZING BUBBLE CAR

Copyright © 2008 Hungry Tiger Press.
All rights reserved.

Book and Cover design by David Maxine.
Illustrations by Howard Heath from the 1907 edition.

The publisher would like to thank Eric Shanower and Bill Thompson for loaning materials from their Baum collections for reproduction in this historic reissue.

ISBN 1-929527-23-3
ISBN 978-1-929527-23-6

This work of fiction by L. Frank Baum was first published in 1907 by The Reilly and Britton Co. of Chicago under the title SAM STEELE'S ADVENTURES IN PANAMA under Baum's pseudonym Captain Hugh Fitzgerald. It was reprinted in 1908 as THE BOY FORTUNE HUNTERS IN PANAMA under the psuedonym Floyd Akers.

The original novel contains a number of racial and ethnic stereotypes that may be considered offensive today. Several potentially offensive words and phrases have been removed from the text. In the interest of historical completeness and for academic research the original unedited portions of the text may be viewed at the URL listed below.

http://hungrytigerpress.com/books/unedited_bubblecar.pdf

HUNGRY TIGER PRESS
5995 Dandridge Lane, Suite 121
San Diego, CA 92115-6575

Visit our website at:
www.hungrytigerpress.com

LIST OF CHAPTERS

CHAPTER ONE
I UNDERTAKE A HAZARDOUS JOURNEY

THE BARK *Nebuchadnesar* came staggering into Chelsea harbor in a very demoralized condition. Her main and mizzen masts were both gone, the bulwarks were smashed in, the poop swept away, and she leaked so badly that all the short-handed crew were nearly ready to drop from the exhausting labor of working the pumps. For after weathering a dreadful storm in which the captain and mate were washed overboard, together with five of the men, those remaining had been forced to rig up a square-sail on the foremast and by hook or crook to work the dismantled hulk into harbor, and this they did from no love of the ship but as a matter of mere self-preservation, the small boats having all been lost or destroyed.

As soon as they dropped anchor in the harbor they fled from the crippled ship and left her to her fate.

It fortunately happened that an agent of the owners, a man named Harlan, lived at Chelsea and was able to take prompt action to save the company's property. The *Nebuchadnesar* was loaded heavily with structural steel work from Birmingham, which had been destined for San Pedro, California, which is the port of entry for the important city of Los Angeles. It was a valuable cargo, and one well worth saving; so Mr. Harlan quickly sent a lot of men aboard to calk the sprung seams and pump her dry, and within twenty-four hours they had her safe from sinking, although she still looked more like a splintered tub than a ship.

And now the agent spent a whole day exchanging telegrams with the chief agents of the Line in New York. It appeared that to unload the heavy structural beams, which were of solid steel, and ship them by rail across the continent would entail a serious loss, the freight rates being enormous for such a distance. There was at the time no other ship procurable to carry the cargo on to its destination. Either the old *Nebuchadnesar* must be made seaworthy again, and sent on its way around the Horn to San Pedro, or the company was in for a tremendous loss.

Harlan was a man of resource and energy. He promptly informed his superiors that he would undertake to fit the ship for sea, and speedily; so he was given permission to "go ahead."

New masts were stepped, the damages repaired, and the bark put in as good condition as possible. But even then it was a sad parody on a ship, and the chances of its ever getting to the port of destination were regarded by all observers as extremely doubtful.

Having done the best in his power, however, Mr. Harlan came to my father and said:

"Captain Steele, I want you to take the *Nebuchadnesar* to San Pedro."

The Captain smiled, and answered with his usual deliberation:

"Thank you, Mr. Harlan; but I can't by any possibility get away this winter."

You see, we were just building our new vessel, the *Seagull*, which was to be our future pride and joy, and my father did not believe the work could progress properly unless he personally inspected every timber and spike that went into her. Just now the builders were getting along finely and during the coming winter all the interior fittings were to be put in. I knew very well that nothing could induce Captain Steele to leave the *Seagull* at this fascinating period of its construction.

Mr. Harlan was very grave and anxious, and spoke frankly of the difficulty he was in.

"You see, sir, my reputation is at stake in this venture," he explained, "and if anything happens to that cargo they will blame me for it. The only way to avoid a heavy loss is to get the old hull into port, and I am aware that to accomplish this task a man of experience and exceptional judgment is required. There is not another captain on the coast that I would so completely and confidently trust with this undertaking as I would you, sir; and we can afford to pay well for the voyage."

My father appreciated the compliment, but it did not alter his resolve.

"Can't be done, Mr. Harlan," he said, pressing the ashes into the bowl of his pipe and looking around the group of intent listeners with a thoughtful expression. "Time was when I'd have liked a job of that sort, because it's exciting to fight a strong ocean with a weak ship. But my whole heart is in the *Seagull,* and I can't an' won't leave her."

Just then his eyes fell upon me and brightened.

"There's no reason, howsomever," he added, "why Sam can't undertake your commission. We won't be likely to need him this winter, at all."

Mr. Harlan frowned; then looked toward me curiously.

"Would you really recommend a boy like Sam for such an important undertaking?" he asked.

"Why not, sir?" replied my father. "Sam's as good a navigator as I am, an' he's a brave lad an' cool-headed, as has been proved. All he lacks is experience in working a ship; but he can take my own mate, Ned Britton, along, and there's not a better sailing-master to be had on the two oceans."

The agent began to look interested. He revolved the matter in his mind for a time and then turned to me and asked, abruptly:

"Would you go, sir?"

I had been thinking, too, for the proposition had come with startling suddenness.

"On one condition," said I.

"What is that?"

"That in case of accident — if, in spite of all our efforts, the old tub goes to the bottom — you will hold me blameless and look as cheerful as possible."

The agent thought that over for what seemed a long time, considering the fact that he was a man of quick judgment and action. But I will acknowledge it was a grave condition I had required, and the man knew even better than I did that under the most favorable circumstances the result of the voyage was more than doubtful. Finally he nodded.

"I do not know of any one I would rather trust," said he. "You are only a boy, Sam Steele; but I've got your record, and I know Ned Britton. Next to getting Captain Steele himself, the combination is as good as I could hope to secure for my company, and I'm going to close with you at once, condition and all."

Britton, who was himself present at this conference, shifted uneasily in his chair.

"I ain't right sure as we can ship a proper crew, sir," he remarked, eyeing me with the characteristic stare of his round, light blue eyes, which were as unreadable as a bit of glass.

"Well, we can try, Ned," I answered, with some concern. "I shall take Nux and Bryonia along, of course, and we won't need over a dozen able seamen."

I must explain that the Nux and Bryonia mentioned were

12

not homeopathic remedies, but two stout, black South Sea Islanders who bore those absurd names and had already proven their loyalty and devotion to me, although they were the especial retainers of my uncle, Naboth Perkins.

"What became of the crew that brought the ship in?" asked my father.

"Deserted, sir, an' dug out quick 's scat," answered Ned.

"Why?"

"Said as nothing but bad luck followed the ship. She were a thirteener, sir, and bound fer to get in trouble."

"How's that?"

"Why, I talked with the second mate, who brung the ship in. He said they had sailed from Liverpool on a Friday, the thirteenth o' the month. There was thirteen aboard; it were the Cap'n's thirteenth voyage; an' the *Nebuchadnesar,* which had thirteen letters in its name — bein' as how it were misspelled by its builders — was thirteen year old to a day. That was bad enough fer a starter, as everybody can guess. Thirteen days out they struck trouble, an' it clung to 'em as desp'rit as their own barnacles. You couldn't hire one o' that crew to go aboard agin, sir, fer love or money."

This dismal revelation struck a chill to all present, except, perhaps, Mr. Harlan and myself. I am superstitious about some things, I acknowledge, but thirteen has for me always been a number luckier than otherwise. However, I knew very well that sailors are obstinate and fearful; so I turned to the agent and said:

"You must paint out that name *Nebuchadnesar* and replace it with any other you like. Do it at once, before we attempt to ship a crew. With that accomplished, Ned won't have much trouble in getting the men he wants."

"I'll do it," replied Mr. Harlan, promptly. "I'll call her

the *Gladys H.*, after my own little daughter. That ought to bring her good luck."

Ned bobbed his head approvingly. It was evident the idea pleased him and removed his most serious objection to the voyage.

"And now," continued the agent, "it is only necessary to discuss terms."

These proved liberal enough, although I must say the money was no factor in deciding me to undertake the voyage. I had been quite fortunate in accumulating a fair share of worldly wealth, and a part of my own snug fortune had gone into our new *Seagull*, of which I was to be one-third owner.

So it was really a desire to be doing something and an irrepressible spirit of adventure that urged me on; for, as my father said, a struggle with old ocean was always full of surprises, and when we had such frail support as the crippled *Nebuchadnesar*, the fight was liable to prove interesting. But that preposterous name was painted out the following day, and before I trod the deck for the first time the bark had been renamed the *Gladys H.*, and was resplendent in fresh paint and new cordage. The old hulk actually looked seaworthy to a superficial observer; but Ned Britton went below and examined her seams carefully and came back shaking his head.

"If the weather holds good and the cargo steady," he said to me, "we may pull through; but if them big iron beams in the hold ever shifts their position, the whole hull 'll open like a sieve."

"Don't whisper that, Ned," I cautioned him. "We've got to take chances."

He was not the man to recoil at taking chances, so he kept a close mouth and in three days secured all the sailors we needed.

They were a fairly good lot, all experienced and

steady, and when I looked them over I was well pleased. One or two who were new to our parts grinned rather disrespectfully when they noted my size and youth; but I paid little attention to that. I was, in reality, a mere boy, and the only wonder is that they consented to sail under my command.

My mate, however, looked every inch the sailor, and won their immediate respect, while my father's ample reputation as a daring and skillful captain caused the men to be lenient in their judgment of his son.

It was to be a long cruise, for Mr. Harlan had instructed me to skirt the coast all the way to Cape Horn, keeping well in to land so that in an emergency I could run the ship ashore and beach her. That would allow us to save the valuable cargo, even if we lost the ship, and that structural steel work was worth a lot of bother, he assured me.

"When you get to the Cape," said the agent, "take your time and wait for good weather to round it. There's no hurry, and by the time you arrive there the conditions ought to be the most favorable of the year. Once in the Pacific, continue to hug the coast up to San Pedro, and then telegraph me for further instructions. Of course you know the consignment is to the contracting firm of Wright & Landers, and when you arrive they will attend to the unloading."

I got my things aboard and found my room very pleasant and of ample size. I took quite a library of books along, for the voyage would surely consume most of the winter. We were liberally provisioned, for the same reason, and our supplies were of excellent quality.

My two black Islanders, Nux and Bryonia, were calmly indifferent to everything except the fact that "Mars' Sam" was going somewhere and would take them along.

Bry was our cook, and a mighty good one, too. With

him in charge of the galley we were sure to enjoy our meals. Nux acted as steward and looked after the officers' cabins. He was wonderfully active and a tower of strength in time of need. Both men I knew I could depend upon at all times, for they were intelligent, active, and would be faithful to the last.

We arranged to sail with the tide on a Wednesday afternoon, the date being the nineteenth of September. On that eventful morning every preparation was reported complete, and I rowed to the shore for a final conference with the agent and a last farewell to my father.

CHAPTER TWO
I SHIP A QUEER PASSENGER

T HE SHIP-YARDS were on this side of the harbor, and presented a busy scene; for besides our own beautiful *Seagull,* whose hull was now nearly complete and so graceful in its lines that it attracted the wondering admiration of every beholder, several other ships were then in the yards in course of construction.

It was in one of the builders' offices that I met my father and Mr. Harlan, and while we were talking a man came in and touched his cap to us, saying:

"May I speak to Captain Steele?" He was about thirty years of age, somewhat thin and lank in appearance, and would have been considered tall had he stood erect instead of stooping at the shoulders. His face was fine and sensitive in expression and his eyes were large and gray but dreamy rather than alert. Gray eyes are usually shrewd; I do not remember ever before seeing so abstracted and visionary a look except in brown or black ones. The man's hair was thick and long and of a light brown — nearly "sandy" — color. He dressed well but carelessly, and was evidently nervous and in a state of suppressed excitement when he accosted us. I noticed that his hands were large and toil-worn, and he clasped and unclasped them constantly as he looked from one to another of our group.

"I am Captain Steele," said my father,

"Then, sir, I desire to ask a favor," was the reply.

"State it, my man."

"I want you to take me and my automobile with you on your voyage to Los Angeles."

Mr. Harlan laughed, and I could not repress a smile myself.

"Then I'm not the Captain Steele you want," said my father. "This is the one you must deal with," pointing his finger in my direction.

The stranger turned, but to my satisfaction seemed in no way surprised or embarrassed by being confronted with a boy.

"It will be a great favor, sir," he continued, earnestly. "I beg you will grant my request,"

"An automobile!" I exclaimed.

"Yes, sir."

"Your request is unusual," I said, in order to decline gracefully, for something about the fellow was strangely appealing. "We are not a passenger ship, but a slow freighter, and we are bound for a long voyage around the Horn."

"Time does not greatly matter," he murmured. "Only one thing really matters at all."

"And that?"

"The expense."

We stared at him, somewhat perplexed.

"Permit me to explain," he went on, still gazing at me alone with his beseeching eyes. "I have invented an automobile—not strictly an automobile, it is true; but for want of a better name I will call it that. I have been years experimenting and building it, for it is all the work of my own hands and the child of my exclusive brain. It is now just finished—complete in every part—but I find that I have exhausted nearly every available dollar of my money. In other words, sir, my machine has bankrupted me."

18

He paused, and catching a wink from Mr. Harlan I said in an amused tone:

"That is an old story, sir."

"You doubt it?"

"No; I mean, that it is quite natural."

"Perhaps," he replied. "You see I had not thought of money; merely of success. But now that at last I have succeeded, I find that I have need of money. My only relative is a rich uncle living at Pasadena, California, who is so eccentric in his disposition that were I to appeal to him for money he would promptly refuse."

"Most rich men have that same eccentricity," I observed.

"But he is quite a genius commercially, and if he saw my machine I am confident he would freely furnish the money I require to erect a manufactory and promote its sale. I assure you, gentlemen," looking vaguely around, "that my machine is remarkable, and an original invention."

We nodded. There was no object in disputing such a modest statement.

"So I wish to get myself and my automobile to Los Angeles, and at the least possible expense. The railroads demand a large sum for freight and fare, and I have not so much money to pay. By accident I learned that your ship is going to the very port I long to reach, and so I hastened to appeal to you to take me. I have only two hundred dollars in my possession—the last, I grieve to say, of my ample inheritance. If you will carry us for that sum to your destination, I shall indeed be grateful for the kindness."

Really, I began to feel sorry for the poor fellow.

"But," said I, "I cannot possibly take you. We sail this afternoon and the hatches are all closed and battened down for the voyage."

"I do not wish the machine put in the hold," he answered, with strange eagerness. "All I ask is a spot in which to place it on the deck — anywhere that will be out of your way. I will make it secure, myself, and take every care of it, so that it will cause you no trouble at all."

"I'm afraid you could not get it to the ship in time."

"It is already loaded upon a flat-boat, which will take it to the *Gladys H.* in an hour, once I have your permission."

I looked at him in astonishment.

"You seem to have considered your request granted in advance," I remarked, with some asperity.

"Not that, sir; I am not impertinent, believe me. But I enquired about Captain Steele and was told that he is a good man and kind. So, that I might lose no time if I obtained your consent, I had the machine loaded on the flat-boat."

Mr. Harlan laughed outright. Acting upon a sudden impulse I turned to him and said:

"May I decide as I please in this matter?"

"Of course, Sam," he replied. "It is your affair, not mine."

I looked at the stranger again. He was actually trembling with anxious uncertainty.

"Very well," I announced, "I will take you."

"For the two hundred dollars?"

"No; I'll carry you for nothing. You may need that extra money at your journey's end."

He took out his handkerchief and wiped his brow, upon which beads of perspiration were standing.

"Thank you, sir," he said, simply.

"But I must warn you of one thing. The bark is not in what we call A-1 condition. If she happens to go to the bottom instead of San Pedro I won't be responsible for your precious machine."

"Very well, sir. I will take as many chances as you do."

"May I ask your name?"

"Moit, sir; Duncan Moit."

"Scotch?"

"By ancestry, Captain. American by birth."

"All right; make haste and get your traps aboard as soon as possible."

"I will. Thank you, Captain Steele."

He put on his cap and walked hurriedly away, and when he had gone both Mr. Harlan and my father rallied me on account of my queer "passenger."

"He looks to me like a crank, Sam," said the agent. "But it's your fireworks, not mine."

"Whatever induced you to take him?" Captain Steele enquired, wonderingly.

"The bare fact that he was so anxious to go," I replied. "He may be a crank on the automobile question, and certainly it is laughable to think of shipping a machine to Los Angeles on a freighter, around the Horn; but the poor fellow seemed to be a gentleman, and he's hard up. It appeared to me no more than a Christian act to help him out of his trouble."

"You may be helping him into trouble, if that confounded cargo of yours takes a notion to shift," observed my father, with a shake of his grizzled head.

"But it's not going to shift, sir," I declared, firmly. "I'm looking for good luck on this voyage, and the chances are I'll find it."

The agent slapped me on the shoulder approvingly.

"That's the way to talk!" he cried. "I'm morally certain, Sam, that you'll land that cargo at San Pedro in safety. I'm banking on you, anyhow, young man."

I thanked him for his confidence, and having bade a last good-bye to my father and my employer I walked away with good courage and made toward my boat, which was waiting for me.

Uncle Naboth was waiting, too, for I found his chubby form squatting on the gunwale.

Uncle Naboth's other name was Mr. Perkins, and he was an important member of the firm of "Steele, Perkins & Steele," being my dead mother's only brother and my own staunch friend. I had thought my uncle in New York until now, and had written him a letter of farewell to his address in that city that very morning.

But here he was, smiling serenely at me as I approached.

"What's this foolishness I hear, Sam?" he demanded, when I had shaken his hand warmly.

"I'm off on a trip around the Horn," said I, "to carry a cargo of building steel to the Pacific coast in that crippled old bark, yonder."

His sharp eye followed mine and rested on the ship.

"Anything in it, my lad?"

"Not much except adventure, Uncle. But it will keep me from growing musty until Spring and the *Seagull* is ready for launching. I'm dead tired of loafing around."

He began to chuckle and cough and choke, but finally controlled himself sufficiently to gasp:

"So 'm I, Sam!"

"You?"

"Tired as blazes. New York's a frost, Sam. Nothin' doin' there that's worth mentionin'. All smug-faced men an' painted-faced women. No sassiety, more policemen than there is sailors, hair-cuts thirty-five cents an' two five-cent drinks fer a quarter. I feel like Alladin an' the Forty Thieves—me bein' Alladin."

"But, Uncle, it wasn't Aladdin that the Forty—"

"Never mind that. Got a spare bunk aboard, Sam?"

I laughed; but there was no use in being surprised at anything Uncle Naboth did.

"I've got a whole empty cabin—second mate's."

"All right. When do we sail?"

"Three o'clock, Uncle Naboth—sharp."

"Very good."

He turned and ambled away toward the town, and, rather thoughtfully, I entered my boat and was rowed out to the *Gladys H.*

CHAPTER THREE
THE MOIT
CONVERTIBLE AUTOMOBILE

T HE FLAT-BOAT came alongside within the hour. On it was a big object covered with soiled canvas and tied 'round and 'round with cords like a package from the grocer. Beside it stood Moit, motionless until the barge made fast and Ned Britton—who at my request had ordered the windlass made ready—had the tackle lowered to hoist it aboard.

Then the inventor directed his men in a clearheaded, composed way that made the task easy enough. The big bundle appeared not so heavy as it looked, and swung up without much strain on the tackle.

I found a place for it just abaft the forecastle, where it would not interfere with the sailors in working the ship. In a brief space of time Duncan Moit had screwed hooks in the planking and lashed his bulky contrivance so firmly to the deck that no ordinary pitch or roll of the ship could possibly affect its security.

Then he carried his trunk and several packages to his cabin, which I had assigned him next my own, and after that I lost sight of him in the responsible duties of our preparations to hoist anchor.

Luncheon was served while we waited for the tide, but there was as yet no sign of Uncle Naboth. I really did not know whether to expect him or not. He might have changed his mind, I reflected; for unless it was a business matter my uncle and partner was wont to be extremely erratic in his decisions. And he had no business at all to join me on this voyage except, as he had said, that he was tired of the land and wished to relieve his restlessness by a smell of salt water.

He was no sailor at all, nor even a navigator; but he had sailed so many years as supercargo and trader that he was seldom contented for long on land, and like myself he dreaded the long wait until Spring when our beautiful new craft would be ready for her maiden trip.

So for a time I thought it probable that he would come alongside; and then I thought it probable he would not. If he ran across Captain Steele, my father was liable to discourage him from making so long and so useless a voyage when no profit was to be had from it. My case was different, for I was a boy still full of a youthful energy and enthusiasm that needed a safety-valve. Moreover, I was pardonably proud of my new position, being for the first time the captain of a ship in name and authority, although I was forced to acknowledge to myself that Ned Britton was the real captain and that without him I would be very helpless indeed.

Two o'clock came, and then three o'clock; but there was no evidence of Uncle Naboth.

I gave a sigh of regret and unfeigned disappointment then, and nodded to Ned to weigh anchor, for the tide was beginning to turn.

My new men worked cheerily and with a will, and soon the anchor was apeak, our mainsail set and we were standing out to sea on our doubtful attempt to round the Horn and reach the blue waters of the Pacific.

We had left the bay and were standing well out from the coast, when I happened to glance over the rail and notice a small launch coming toward us from the harbor at full speed. They were unable to signal from that distance, but I brought a powerful glass and soon made out the form of Uncle Naboth standing upright in the middle of the little craft and gracefully waving a red handkerchief.

I had Ned luff and lay to, laughing to think how nearly the little uncle had missed us, and before long the launch covered the distance between us and came alongside.

Uncle Naboth was gorgeous in appearance. He was dressed in a vividly checked suit and wore a tourist cap perched jauntily atop his iron-gray locks. His shirt bosom was wonderfully pleated, his shoes of shiney patent-leather, and he wore yellow kid gloves that wrinkled dreadfully. Moreover — the greatest wonder of all, to me — my uncle was smoking a big, fat cigar instead of his accustomed corn-cob pipe, and he had a kodak slung over one shoulder and a marine-glass over the other.

First of all my uncle sent his traps up the side. Then he began a long but calm argument with the crew of the launch, who were greatly excited, and this might have continued indefinitely had not Ned become impatient and yelled a warning that he was about to tack. At this Uncle Naboth thrust some money in the hand of the skipper and leisurely ascended the ladder while a chorus of curses and threats fell upon his unheeding ears.

"Nearly missed you, Sam, didn't I?" he said, nodding cheerfully as the sails filled and we headed into the breeze again. "Close shave, but no alum or bay-rum."

"What made you late, Uncle?"

"Had to do a lot to git my outfit ready," he said, puffing his cigar, smoothing out his gloves and at the same time casting a critical eye over the deck. "First time in my life, nevvy, that I've went to sea on a pleasure-trip. No business to look after, no worry, no figgerin'. Jest sailin' away o'er the deep blue sea with a jolly crew is the life for me. Eh, Sam?"

"Right you are, Uncle. You're just a passenger, and a

mighty welcome one. I'm glad you caught us."

"Stern chase, but not a long one. What do you s'pose, Sam? I had to pay them pirates in that half-grown steamboat thirty dollars to get me aboard."

"Thirty dollars!"

"Dreadful, wasn't it? And then they wanted sixty. Took me for a tourist gent 'cause I looked the part. But I was bound to come, an' they was onto my anxiousness, so it might be expected as they'd soak me good an' plenty. Where'd you say you was bound for, Sam?"

"Down the coast, around the Horn, and up the Pacific to San Pedro."

"Sounds interestin'."

His bright little eye had been observant.

"What's aboard, my lad?"

"Steel beams for some new buildings in Los Angeles."

"Loaded rather heavy, ain't she?"

"Top heavy, Uncle."

"H-m-m. Not any too tight, either, I take it. Hull old an' rotten; plenty o' paint to cover up the worm-holes."

"Exactly, sir."

"Will you make it, Sam?"

"Can't say, Uncle Naboth. But I'll try."

"Cargo insured?"

"No; that's the worst of it. The owners insure themselves, because the tub won't pass at Lloyd's. If we sink it's a big loss. So we mustn't sink."

"Iron won't float, nevvy."

"I'm going to hug the coast, mostly. If trouble comes I'll beach her. You may be in for a long cruise, Uncle."

He nodded quite pleasantly.

"That's all right. I take it we'll manage to get home by spring, an' that's time enough fer us both. But I can see she ain't a race-hoss, Sam, my boy."

Indeed, the ship was not behaving at all to suit me. With a favorable breeze and an easy sea the miserable old hulk was sailing more like a water-logged raft than a modern merchantman.

Her sails and cordage were new and beautiful, and her paint spick and span; but I noticed my sailors wagging their heads with disappointment as the *Gladys H.* labored through the water.

Uncle Naboth chuckled to himself and glanced at me as if he thought it all a good joke, and I the only victim. But I pretended to pay no attention to him. Being, as he expressed it, a "loafin' land-lubber," I installed him in the last of the roomy cabins aft, all of which opened into the officers' mess-room. Ned Britton had the cabin opposite mine, and Mr. Perkins the one opposite to that occupied by Duncan Moit. For my part, I was pleased enough to have such good company on a voyage that promised to be unusually tedious.

Moit had kept well out of our way until everything was snug and ship-shape, and then he came on deck and stood where he could keep a tender eye on his precious machine. I introduced him to Uncle Naboth and the two "passengers" shook hands cordially and were soon conversing together in a friendly manner.

I had decided to take my sailors into my confidence in the very beginning, so I called all hands together and made them a brief speech.

"My lads," said I, "we need not look forward to a very good voyage, for you have doubtless discovered already that the *Gladys H.* is not a greyhound. To be honest with you, she's old and leaky, and none too safe. But she's got a valuable cargo aboard, that must be safe delivered if we can manage it, and we are all of us well paid to do our duty by the owners. My instructions are to hug the land

and make a harbor if bad weather comes. At the worst we can run the ship on the shingle and save the cargo in that way — for the cargo is worth a dozen such tubs. It's a somewhat risky undertaking, I know, and if any of you don't like your berths I'll put you ashore at the first likely place and you can go home again. But if you are willing to stick to me, I'll take as good care of you as I can, and your money is sure because the Interocean Forwarding Company is back of us and good for every penny. What do you say, my lads?"

They were a good-natured lot, and appreciated my frankness. After a little conference together the boatswain declared they were all content to see the venture to the end and do the best they could under the circumstances. So a mutual understanding was established from the beginning, and before the end came I had cause to be proud of every man aboard.

The weather was warm and pleasant and as I sat with our passengers and Ned on the deck in the afternoon Uncle Naboth got his eye on the overgrown grocery package and said to Moit :

"What sort of an automobile have you got?"

The man had been dreaming, but he gave a start and his eyes lighted with sudden interest. The abstracted mood disappeared.

"It is one of my own invention, sir," he replied.

"What do you call it?"

"The Moit Convertible Automobile."

"Heh? Convertible?"

"Yes, sir."

"I guess," said Uncle Naboth, "I'm up agin it. 'Convertible' is a word I don't jest catch the meaning of. Latin's a little rusty, you know; so long since I went to school."

"It means," said Moit, seriously, "that the machine is equally adapted to land and water."

My uncle stared a little, then looked away and began to whistle softly. Ned Britton sighed and walked to the rail as if to observe our motion. For my part, I had before entertained a suspicion that the poor fellow was not quite right in his mind, so I was not surprised. But he appeared gentlemanly enough, and was quite in earnest; so, fearing he might notice the rather pointed conduct of my uncle and Ned, I made haste to remark with fitting gravity:

"That is a very desirable combination, Mr. Moit, and a great improvement on the ordinary auto."

"Oh, there is nothing ordinary about the machine, in any way," he responded, quickly. "Indeed, it is so different from all the other motor vehicles in use that it cannot properly be termed an automobile. Some time I intend to provide an appropriate name for my invention, but until now the machine itself has occupied my every thought."

"To be sure," I said, rather vaguely.

"Most automobiles," began my uncle, lying back in his chair and giving me a preliminary wink, "is only built to go on land, an' balks whenever they gets near a repair shop. I was tellin' a feller the other day in New York, who was becalmed in the middle of the street, that if he'd only put a sail on his wagon and wait for a stiff breeze, he could tell all the repair men to go to thunder!"

"But this has nothing to do with Mr. Moit's invention," I said, trying not to smile. "Mr. Moit's automobile is different."

"As how?" asked my uncle.

Mr. Moit himself undertook to reply.

"In the first place," said he, his big eyes looking straight through me with an absorbed expression, as if I were invisible, "I do not use the ordinary fuel for locomotion.

Gasoline is expensive and dangerous, and needs constant replenishing. Electricity is unreliable, and its storage very bulky. Both these forces are crude and unsatisfactory. My first thought was to obtain a motive power that could be relied upon at all times, that was inexpensive and always available. I found it in compressed air."

"Oh!" ejaculated Uncle Naboth.

I am sure he knew less about automobiles than I did, for I owned a small machine at home and had driven it some while on shore. But Mr. Perkins prided himself on being familiar with all modern inventions, and what he did not know from personal experience he was apt to imagine he knew.

"Compressed air," he observed, oracularly, "is what blows the sails of a ship."

The inventor turned on him a look of wonder.

"This seems to me like a clever idea," I hastened to say. "But I can't see exactly, sir, how you manage to use compressed air for such a purpose."

"I have a storage tank," Moit answered, "which is constantly replenished by the pumps as fast as the air is exhausted, which of course only occurs while the machine is in action."

"But you need something to start the engines," I suggested. "Do you use gasoline for that purpose?"

"No, sir. I have a glycerine explosive which is so condensed that an atom is all that is required to prime the engines. In a little chamber that contains about a pint I can carry enough explosive to last me for a year. And wherever there is air I have power that is perpetual."

"That's great!" cried Uncle Naboth, with an enthusiasm so plainly assumed that Ned and I had much ado to keep from laughing outright.

"In other ways," continued Duncan Moit, "I have made

marked improvements upon the ordinary motor car. Will you allow me, gentlemen, to show you my machine, and to explain it to you?"

We were glad enough of this diversion, even Ned Britton, who could not have run a sewing-machine, being curious to examine our crazy passenger's invention.

Moit at once began to untie the cords and remove the soiled canvas, which consisted of parts of worn-out sails stitched clumsily together. But when this uninviting cover was withdrawn we saw with astonishment a machine of such beauty, completeness and exquisite workmanship that our exclamations of delight were alike spontaneous and genuine.

Moit might be mad, but as a mechanic he was superb, if this was indeed a creation of his own hands.

An automobile? Well, it had four massive wheels with broad rubber tires, a steering gear (of which only the wheel was visible) and a body for the passengers to ride in; but otherwise the world-pervading auto-fiend would not have recognized the thing.

It seemed to be all of metal—a curious metal of a dull silver hue—not painted or polished in any place, but so finely constructed that every joint and fitting appeared perfect. It was graceful of design, too, although the body was shaped like the hull of a boat, with the wheels so placed that the structure was somewhat more elevated from the ground than ordinarily. This body was about a foot in thickness, having an inner and outer surface composed of beautifully rivetted plates of the strange metal.

Moit explained that part of this space was used for vacuum chambers, which were kept exhausted by the pumps when required and made the machine wonderfully light. Also, within what corresponded with the gunwale of a boat, were concealed the parts of the adjustable

top, which, when raised into position and hooked together, formed a dome-shaped cover for the entire body.
These parts were almost entirely of glass, in which a fine
wire netting had been imbedded, so that while the riders
could see clearly on all sides, any breakage of the glass was
unlikely to occur. In any event it could only crack, as the
netting would still hold the broken pieces in place.

The engines were in a front-chamber of the body. There
were four of them, each no bigger than a gallon jug; but
Moit assured us they were capable of developing twenty-
five horse-power each, or a total of one hundred horse-
power, owing to the wonderful efficiency of the compressed air. All the other machinery was similarly condensed in size and so placed that the operator could reach
instantly any part of it.

The entrance was at either side or at the back, as one
preferred, but the seats were arranged in a circle around
the body, with the exception of the driver's chair. So
roomy was the car that from six to eight passengers could
be carried with comfort, or even more in case of emergency.

All of these things were more easily understood by
observation than I can hope to explain them with the pen.
Perhaps I have omitted to describe them to you as clearly
as I should; but I must plead in extenuation a lack of
mechanical knowledge. That you will all ride in similar
cars some day I have no doubt, and then you will understand all the details that I, a plain sailor, have been
forced to ignore because of my ignorance of mechanics.

"But," said Uncle Naboth, whose eyes were fairly
bulging with amazement, "I don't yet see what drives the
blamed thing through water."

Moit smiled for almost the first time since I had known
him, and the smile was one of triumphant pride.

He entered the automobile, touched some buttons, and with a whirring sound a dozen little scoop-shaped flanges sprang from the rim of each wheel. There was no need for farther explanation. We could see at once that in water the four wheels now became paddle-wheels, and their rapid revolution would no doubt drive the machine at a swift pace.

The paddles were cleverly shaped, being made of the same metal employed everywhere in the construction of this astonishing invention, and they stood at just the right angle to obtain the utmost power of propulsion.

"Aluminum?" questioned Mr. Perkins, pointing to the metal.

"No, sir. This is perhaps my most wonderful discovery, and you will pardon me if I say it is a secret which I am unwilling at this time to divulge. But I may tell you that I have found an alloy that is unequalled in the known world for strength, durability and lightness. It weighs a little more than pure aluminum, but has a thousand times its tensile strength. You may test one of these blades, which seem to the eye to be quite delicate and fragile."

Uncle Naboth leaned over and gingerly tested one of the wheel blades with his thumb and finger. Then he exerted more strength. Finally he put his heel upon it and tried to bend it with the weight of his body. It resisted all efforts with amazing success.

And now the inventor pushed some other buttons, or keys, and the metal blades all receded and became once more a part of the rims of the wheels.

"When we get to San Pedro, gentlemen," said he, "it will give me pleasure to take you for a ride in my machine, both on land and water. Then you will be sure to appreciate its perfection more fully."

He began to replace the canvas cover, apologizing as much to his beloved machine as to us for its shabbiness.

34

"All of my money was consumed by the machine itself," he explained, "and I was forced to use this cloth to make a cover, which is needed only to protect my invention from prying eyes. The metal will never rust nor corrode."

"Is this material, this alloy, easy to work?" I asked.

He shook his head.

"It is very difficult," he returned. "Steel crumbles against it with discouraging readiness, so that my tools were all of the same metal, annealed and hardened. Even these had to be constantly replaced. You must not imagine, sir, that I obtained all of this perfection at the first trial. I have been years experimenting."

"So I imagine, Mr. Moit."

"By a fortunate coincidence," he went on, dreamily, "my money, which I had inherited from my father, lasted me until all the work was complete. I had thought of nothing but my machine, and having at last finished it and made thorough tests to assure myself that it was as nearly perfect as human skill can make it, I awoke to find myself bankrupt and in debt. By selling my tools, my workshop, and everything else I possessed except the machine itself I managed to pay my indebtedness and have two hundred dollars left. This was not enough to get myself and my car shipped to California by rail; so I was at my wits' end until you, sir," turning to me, "kindly came to my rescue."

During the pause that followed he finished covering up his machine, and then Uncle Naboth asked, bluntly:

"If you are sure the blamed thing will work, why didn't you run it overland to California? That has been done more 'n once, I'm told, and as you use compressed air the expense wouldn't be a circumstance."

That had occurred to me too, and I awaited the man's reply with much curiosity.

"Sir," he answered, "you must not forget that I have devoted years to this work—years of secret and constant toil—and that my whole heart is involved in the success of my perfected machine. But you can readily understand that I have not dared to patent it, or any of its parts, until all was complete; for an imperfect patent not only fails to protect one, but in this case it would give other designers of automobiles the ideas I had originated. A patent is never a safeguard if it can be improved or stolen. As I have said, when at last my work was finished I had no money with which to obtain patents, of which no less than nineteen are required to protect me."

"And have you, at this time, no patents at all?" I asked, surprised at such neglect.

He shook his head.

"Not one. There, gentlemen, stands one of the most important mechanical inventions the world has ever known, and its inventor has no protection whatever—as yet. If I attempted to run the machine overland to the Pacific coast, a dozen automobile experts would see it and promptly steal my ideas. Such a risk was too great to run. I must manage to reach my rich and selfish uncle, prove to him how wonderful my invention is, offer him a half interest in it, and so procure the money to protect it and to establish a manufactory. Do you understand now why I have acted in so puzzling a way—puzzling, at least, to one not aware of my dilemma?"

"It is quite clear to me," I replied, beginning to think my passenger was not mad, after all. "But have you not been foolish to confide all this to us?"

He smiled pleasantly, and the smile made his face really attractive.

"I am not especially stupid, believe me," said he, "and I am a fair judge of human nature. You will pardon me if I say that not a man on this ship is at all dangerous to me."

"How is that?" I asked, slightly discomfitted.

"No man among you is competent to steal my invention," he asserted, coolly, "even if you were disposed to do so, which I doubt. It would require a dishonest person who is a mechanical expert, and while there are many such between Chelsea and California, I am sure there is none on this ship who would wrong me, even if he possessed the power. I feel entirely secure, gentlemen, in your company."

This was diplomatic, at least, for we were naturally pleased at the tribute to our good faith, even if inclined to resent the disparagement of our mechanical genius. However, we regarded Duncan Moit in a more friendly light and with vastly increased respect from that time forth.

It was growing dark by this time, and presently Nux announced that dinner was served. So we repaired to the mess cabin, and while testing Bryonia's superb talents as a cook beguiled the hour by canvassing the future possibilities of the Moit Convertible Automobile.

CHAPTER FOUR
WE COME TO GRIEF

ORTUNE SEEMED TO favor the voyage of the *Gladys H.*
All the way to Hatteras the weather was delightful
and the breeze fresh and constant. There was not a
moment when the sails were not bulging to some extent
and in spite of the old ship's labored motion we made
excellent time.

However, I followed my instructions, keeping well in
toward the coast, and so crept steadily down to Key West.

Here an important proposition confronted us: whether
to enter the Gulf of Mexico and follow its great circle near
to the shore—a method that would require weeks—or run
across to Cuba and then attempt the passage of the
Caribbean by the short cut to Colon or Porto Bella. We had
canvassed this alternative before I left harbor; but Mr.
Harlan had maintained that I must decide the question for
myself, being guided by the actions of the bark and the
condition of the weather.

Both these requirements seemed favorable for the short
cut. The ship had behaved so far much better than I had
expected, and the good weather seemed likely to hold for
some time longer.

So after a conference with Ned Britton—for Uncle
Naboth refused to "mix up in the business" or even to
offer an opinion—I decided to take the chances and follow
the shortest route. After reaching Colon I would keep close
to land way down to the Horn.

So we stood out to sea, made Cuba easily, and skirted
its western point to the Isles de Pinos. Still the skies were

clear and the breeze favorable, and with good courage we headed south in a bee-line for Colon.

And now we were in the Caribbean, that famous sea whose very name breathes romance. It recalls to us the earliest explorers, the gold seekers and buccaneers, the fact that scarce an inch of its rippling surface is unable to boast some tragedy or adventure in the days of the Spanish Main, when ships of all nations thronged the waters of the West Indies.

For three whole days luck was our bedfellow; then, as Uncle Naboth drily remarked, it "went a fishin' " and left us to take care of ourselves.

With gentle sighs our hitherto faithful breeze deserted us and our sails flapped idly for a time and then lay still, while the ship floated upon a sheet of brilliant blue glass, the tropic sun beat fiercely down upon us, and all signs of life and animation came to an end.

No sailor is partial to calms. A gale he fights with a sense of elation and a resolve to conquer; a favoring breeze he considers his right; but a glassy sea and listless, drooping sails are his especial horror. Nevertheless, he is accustomed to endure this tedium and has learned by long experience how best to enliven such depressing periods.

Our men found they possessed a violinist—not an unskilled fiddler by any means—and to his accompanying strains they sang and danced like so many happy children.

Uncle Naboth and Ned Britton played endless games of penocle under the deck awning and I brought out my favorite books and stretched myself in a reclining chair to enjoy them.

Duncan Moit paced deliberately up and down for the first two days, engrossed in his own musings; then he decided to go over his machine and give it a careful examination. He removed the cover, started his engines, and let them perform for the amusement of the amazed sailors, who formed a curious but respectful group around him.

Finally they cleared a space on the deck and Moit removed the guy-ropes that anchored his invention and ran his auto slowly up and down, to the undisguised delight of the men. He would allow six or eight to enter the car and ride — sixteen feet forward, around the mainmast, and sixteen feet back again — and it was laughable to watch the gravity of their faces as they held fast to the edge, bravely resolving to endure the dangers of this wonderful mode of locomotion. Not one had ever ridden in an automobile before, and although Moit merely allowed it to crawl over its confined course, the ride was a strange and fascinating experience to them.

I must allow that the performances of this clever machine astonished me. The inventor was able to start it from his seat, by means of a simple lever, and it was always under perfect control. The engines worked so noiselessly that you had to put your ear close in order to hear them at all, and the perfection of the workmanship could not fail to arouse my intense admiration.

"If this new metal is so durable as you claim," I said to Moit, "the machine ought to last for many years."

"My claim is that it is practically indestructible," he answered, in a tone of conviction.

"But you have still the tire problem," I remarked. "A puncture will put you out of business as quickly as it would any other machine."

"A puncture!" he exclaimed. "Why, these tires cannot puncture, sir."

"Why not?"

"They are not inflated."

"What then?"

"It is another of my inventions, Mr. Steele. Inside each

casing is a mass of sponge-rubber, of a peculiarly resilient and vigorous character. And within the casing itself is embedded a net of steel wire, which will not allow the vulcanized rubber to be cut to any depth. The result is an excellent tire that cannot be punctured and has great permanency."

"You do not seem to have overlooked any important point," I observed, admiringly.

"Ah, that is the one thing that now occupies my mind," he responded, quickly. "That is why I have been testing the machine today, even in the limited way that is alone possible. I am haunted by the constant fear that I *have* overlooked some important point, which another might discover."

"And have you found such a thing?"

"No; to all appearances the device is perfect. But who can tell what may yet develop?"

"Not I," with a smile; "you have discounted my mechanical skill already. To my mind the invention seems in every way admirable, Mr. Moit."

For nine days we lay becalmed, with cloudless skies above and a tranquil sea around us. During the day we rested drowsily in the oppressive heat, but the nights were always cooler and myriads of brilliant stars made it nearly as light as day. Ned had taken in every yard of canvas except a square sail which he rigged forward, and he took the added precaution to lash every movable thing firmly to its place.

"After this, we've got to expect ugly weather," he announced; and as he knew the Caribbean well this preparation somewhat dismayed me. I began to wish we had entered the Gulf of Mexico and made the roundabout trip; but it was too late for regrets now, and we must make the best of our present outlook.

41

Personally I descended into the hold and examined with care the seams, finding that the calking had held securely so far and that we were as right and tight as when we had first sailed. But even this assurance was not especially encouraging, for we had met with no weather that a canoe might not have lived through without shipping more than a few drops of sea.

The ninth day was insufferably hot, and the evening brought no relief. Ned Britton's face looked grave and worried, and I overheard him advising Duncan Moit to add several more anchor ropes to those that secured his machine.

We awaited the change in the weather anxiously enough, and toward midnight the stars began to be blotted out until shortly a black pall overhung the ship. The air seemed vibrant and full of an electric feel that drew heavily upon one's nerves; but so far there had been no breath of wind.

At last, when it seemed we could wait no longer, a distant murmur was heard, drawing ever nearer and louder until its roar smote our ears like a discharge of artillery. The ship began to roll restlessly, and then the gale and the waves broke upon us at the same instant and with full force.

Heavily weighted and lazy as the bark was, she failed to rise to the first big wave, which washed over her with such resistless power that it would have swept every living soul away had we not clung desperately to the rigging. It seemed to me that I was immersed in a wild, seething flood for several minutes; but they must have been seconds, instead, for presently the water was gone and the wind endeavoring to tear me from my hold.

The square sail held, by good luck, and the ship began to stagger onward, bowing her head deep and submitting to constant floods that washed her from end to end. There was not much that could be done to ease her, and the fervid excitement of those first hours kept us all looking after our personal safety. Along we went, scudding before the gale, which maintained its intensity unabated and fortunately drove us along the very course we had mapped out.

The morning relieved the gloom, but did not lessen the force of the storm. The waves were, rolling pretty high, and all faces were serious or fearful, according to the disposition of their owners. In our old *Saracen,* or even the *Flipper,* I would not have minded the blow or the sea, but here was a craft of a different sort, and I did not know how she might stand such dreadful weather.

I got Ned into the cabin, where we stood like a couple of drenched rats and discussed the situation. On deck our voices could not be heard.

"Are the small boats ready to launch?" I asked.

"All ready, sir; but I doubt if they'd live long," he replied. "However, this 'ere old hulk seems to be doin' pretty decent. She lies low, bein' so heavy loaded, an' lets the waves break over her. That saves her a good deal of strain, Sam. If she don't spring a leak an' the cargo holds steady, we'll get through all right."

"Tried the pumps?"

"Yes; only bilge, so far."

"Very good. How long will the gale last?"

"Days, perhaps, in these waters. There's no rule to go by, as I knows of. It'll just blow till it blows itself out."

He went on deck again, keeping an eye always on the ship and trying to carry just enough canvas to hold her steady.

Duncan Moit and Uncle Naboth kept to the cabin and were equally unconcerned. The latter was an old voyager and realized that it was best to be philosophical; the former had never been at sea before and had no idea of our danger.

On the third morning of this wild and persistent tempest the boatswain came to where Ned and I clung to the rigging and said:

"She's leaking, sir."

"Badly?"

"Pretty bad, sir."

"Get the pumps manned, Ned," said I; "I'll go below and investigate."

I crawled into the hold through the forecastle cubby, as we dared not remove the hatches. I took along a sailor to carry the lantern, and we were not long in making the discovery that the *Gladys H.* was leaking like a sieve. Several of the seams that Mr. Harlan had caused to be calked so carefully had reopened and the water was spurting through in a dozen streams.

I got back to my cabin and made a careful examination of the chart. According to my calculations we could not be far from the coast of Panama. If I was right, another six hours would bring us to the shore; but I was not sure of my reckoning since that fearful gale had struck us. So the question whether or no the ship could live six hours longer worried me considerably, for the pumps were of limited capacity and the water was gaining on us every minute.

I told Uncle Naboth our difficulty, and Duncan Moit, who stood by, listened to my story with lively interest.

"Will you try to beach her, Sam?" enquired my uncle, with his usual calmness.

"Of course, sir, if we manage to float long enough to reach the land. That is the best I can hope for now. By good luck the coast of Panama is low and marshy, and if we can drive the tub aground there the cargo may be saved to the owners."

"Ain't much of a country to land in, Sam; is it?"

"Not a very lovely place, Uncle, I'm told."

"It's where they're diggin' the canal, ain't it?"

"I believe so."

"Well, we may get a chance to see the ditch. This 'ere travellin' is full of surprises, Mr. Moit. I never thought to 'a' brung a guide book o' Panama, or we could tell exactly where they make the hats."

The inventor appeared ill at ease. I could understand the man's disappointment and anxiety well enough. To beach his beloved machine on a semi-barbarous, tropical shore was not what he had anticipated, and I had time to feel sorry for him while thinking upon my own troubles.

He followed me on deck, presently, and I saw him take a good look at the sea and shake his head despondently. The Convertible Automobile might work in ordinary water, but it was not intended for such mammoth waves as these.

Then he watched the men at the pumps. They worked with a will, but in that cheerless way peculiar to sailors when they are forced to undertake this desperate duty. The ocean was pushing in and they were trying to keep it out; and such a pitiful struggle usually results in favor of the ocean.

Suddenly Moit conceived a brilliant idea. He asked for a length of hose, and when it was brought he threw off the covering of his machine and succeeded in attaching the hose to his engines. The other end we dropped into the hold, and presently, despite the lurching and plunging of the ship, the engines started and a stream the full size of the hose was sucked up and sent flowing into the scruppers. It really did better work than the ship's pumps, and I am now positive that this clever arrangement was all that enabled us to float until we made the coast.

In the afternoon, while the gale seemed to redouble its force, we sighted land — low, murky and uninteresting, but nevertheless land — and made directly for it.

Darkness came upon us swiftly, but we held our course, still pumping for dear life and awaiting with tense nerves the moment of impact.

What this shore, of which we had caught a glimpse, might be like I did not know, more than that it was reported low and sandy at the ocean's edge and marshy in the interior. There were a few rocky islands at the south of the isthmus, and there might be rocks or breakers at any point, for all we knew. If the ship struck one of these we were surely doomed.

On and on we flew, with blackness all round us, until on a sudden the bow raised and our speed slackened so abruptly that we were all thrown prostrate upon the deck. The mainmast snapped and fell with a deafening crash, and slowly the ship rolled to starboard until the deck stood at a sharp angle, and trembled a few brief moments, and then lay still.

The voyage of the *Gladys H.* was at an end.

CHAPTER FIVE
MAKING THE
BEST OF IT

A RE YOU THERE, Sam?"
"Yes, Ned."
"Safe and sound?"
"I think so."

Overhead the wind still whistled, but more moderately; around me I could hear the men stirring, with an occasional groan. We had come from the tempest-tossed seas into a place of comparative quiet, which just now was darker than the pocket of Erebus.

I found the after cabin and slid down the steps, which inclined sidewise. Inside however, the hanging lamps had withstood the shock and still cast a dim light over the room. I found Uncle Naboth reclining upon a bench with his feet braced against the table, while he puffed away complacently at one of his enormous cigars.

"Stopped at a way station, Sam?" he enquired.

"So it appears, Uncle."

"Any damage?"

"Can't tell, yet. Were you hurt?"

He exhibited a great lump on his forehead, but smiled sweetly.

"You should 'a' seen me dive under the table, Sam. It were a reg'lar circus, with me the chief acrobat. Where are we?"

"I'm going to find out."

I unhooked both the lanterns and started up the companion-way with them. Rather than remain in the dark, Uncle brought himself and his cigar after me.

I gave Ned one of the lights and we began to look about us. Duncan Moit lay unconscious beside his machine, the engines of which were still running smoothly. I threw back the lever and stopped them, and then a couple of seamen carried the inventor into the cabin. Black Nux had lighted another lantern, and with my uncle's assistance undertook to do what he could to restore the injured man.

Ned and I slid aft and found the stern still washed by a succession of waves that dashed over it. Walking the deck was difficult because the ship listed from stem to stern and from port to starboard. Her bow was high and dry on a sand-bar — or such I imagined it to be — but it was only after I had swung a lantern up a halyard of the foremast, so that its dim rays would illumine the largest possible area, that I discovered we had plunged straight into a deep inlet of the coast. On one side of us appeared to be a rank growth of tangled shrubs or underbrush; on the other was the outline of a forest. Ahead was clear water, but its shallow depth had prevented our proceeding farther inland.

Either the gale had lessened perceptibly or we did not feel it so keenly in our sheltered position. An examination of the men showed that one of them had broken an arm and several others were badly bruised; but there were no serious casualties.

The ship was now without any motion whatever, being fast on the bottom of the inlet. The breakers that curled over the stern did her no damage, and these seemed to be gradually lessening in force.

Ned sent his tired men to their bunks and with the assistance of Bryonia, who was almost as skillful in surgery as in cooking, prepared to set the broken arm and attend to those who were the most bruised.

I went to the cabin again, and found that Uncle Naboth and Nux had been successful in restoring Duncan Moit, who was sitting up and looking around him with a dazed expression. I saw he was not much hurt, the fall having merely stunned him for the time being.

"The machine—the machine!" he was muttering, anxiously.

"It's all right, sir," I assured him. "I shut down the engines, and she seems to have weathered the shock in good shape."

He seemed relieved by this report, and passed his hand across his brow as if to clear his brain.

"Where are we?" was his next query.

"No one knows, sir. But we are landed high and dry, and I'm almost sure it is some part of the coast of Panama. To-morrow morning we can determine our location more accurately. But now, Mr. Moit, I recommend that you tumble into your bunk and get all the rest you can before daybreak."

The strain of the last few days had been severe upon all of us, and now that the demand for work or vigilance was removed we found that our strength had been overtaxed. I left Ned to set a watch, and sought my own bed, on which I stretched myself to fall asleep in half a minute.

"Wake up, Mars' Sam," said Nux, shaking me. "Breakfas' ready, seh."

I rubbed my eyes and sat up. The sun was streaming through the cabin window, which was on the port side. Around me was a peculiar silence which contrasted strongly with the turmoil that had so long buffeted my ears. The gale had passed on and left us to count the mischief it had caused.

"What time is it, Nux?"

"Eight o'clock, Mars' Sam."

I sprang up, now fully conscious of the night's tragedy, which sleep had for a time driven from my mind. Nux stood with my basin and towel and his calmness encouraged me to bathe before I went on deck.

In the mess-cabin I found that the table legs had been propped up with boxes to hold it level, and that a hot breakfast had been prepared and was now steaming on the table. Around the board were gathered Ned Britton, Uncle Naboth and Duncan Moit, all busily engaged in eating. They greeted me cheerfully and bade me sit down and join them.

"How is everything, Ned?" I enquired, anxiously.

"Bad as can be, an' right as a trivet, Sam," he replied. "The *Gladys H.* 'll never float again. Her bottom's all smashed in, an' she's fast in the mud till she goes to pieces an' makes kindlin'-wood for the Indians."

"Then the cargo is safe, for the present?"

"To be sure. It can't get lost, 'cause it's a chunk o' steel, and the ship's planks 'll hold it in place for a long time. It'll get good and soaked, but I've noticed it's all painted to keep it from rustin'. This ain't San Pedro, whatever else it is, and the voyage has miscarried a bit; but them beams is a good deal better off here than at the bottom o' the sea, so I take it we've done the best we could by the owners."

I sat down and took the coffee Nux poured for me.

"How about the crew?" I asked. "Are the men all right?"

"Nobody hurt but Dick Lombard, and his arm 'll mend nicely."

"Have you any idea where we are, Ned?"

"Stuck in a river, somewhere. Wild country all around us, but I guess we can find a way out. Lots o' provisions and a good climate. We may say as we're in luck, Sam."

I shook my head dismally. It did not appear to me that luck had especially favored us. To be sure, we might have gone to the bottom of the Caribbean in the gale; but it struck me we had landed the cargo in an awkward place for the owners as well as for ourselves. Mr. Harlan would have done better had he not taken the long chance of our making the voyage to San Pedro successfully.

"Well, I cannot see that we have failed in our duty, in any way," I remarked, as cheerfully as I could, "so we may as well make the best of it."

"This bein' a tourist, an' travellin' fer pleasure," said Uncle Naboth, "is more fun than a kickin' mule. Sam's got to worry, 'cause he's paid fer it; but we passengers can look on an' enjoy ourselves. Eh, Mr. Moit?"

"It is a serious situation for me," replied the inventor. "Think of it, gentlemen! The most wonderful piece of mechanism the world has yet known is stranded in a wilderness, far from civilization."

"That is your own fault," remarked Ned, bluntly.

"Not that, sir; it is fate."

"The machine is all right," said I. "You will have no trouble to save it."

"As for that, I must, of course, make the best of the adverse circumstances that have overtaken me," he replied, with more composure than I had expected. "It is not my nature to be easily discouraged, else I could never have accomplished what I have in the perfection of any inventions. My greatest regret, at this moment, is that the world will be deprived, for a longer period than I had intended, of the benefits of my Convertible Automobile."

"Having never known its excellent qualities, sir, the world can wait," asserted Uncle Naboth, philosophically. I have noticed one can be quite philosophical over another's difficulties.

Having hurried through my breakfast, which our faithful Bryonia had prepared most excellently in spite of the fact that his galley was at an angle of nearly forty-five degrees, I went on deck to obtain for the first time a clear view of our surroundings.

The tide had changed and the wind fallen. We lay in the center of a placid river — high and dry, as Ned had said — with the current gently rippling against our bow. Not more than ten yards to the right was a low, marshy bank covered with scrub underbrush of a tropical character. On our left, however, and some fifty yards distant, lay a well defined bank marking the edge of the stately forest which I had observed the night before. The woodland gradually sloped upward from the river, and above it, far to the south, a formidable range of mountains was visible.

Between us and this left bank the water seemed a fair depth, but it was quite shallow on our right. It seemed wonderful that any gale could have sent so big a ship so far up the river; but I remembered that the billows had followed us in, and doubtless their power alone had urged us forward.

Here we were, anyway, and here the *Gladys H.* must remain until demolished by time, tide or human endeavor.

For the rest, the air was warm and pleasant, with a blue sky overhead. Aside from the loss that would follow the salvage of the valuable cargo, we had good reason to thank Providence for our fortunate escape from death.

I felt that I had done as much to promote the interests of the owners as any man could do; but the conditions had been adverse, and the responsibility was now theirs, and not mine.

The gravest part of the situation, so far as I was personally concerned, was to get my men into some civilized port where they could find an opportunity to get home again. Also I must notify Mr. Harlan, by cable, and that as soon as possible, of the location and condition of his cargo. The loss of the ship I knew would matter little to him, as he had asserted this several times.

And now to solve the problem of our location. I had reason to believe that we had not varied to any great extent from the course my chart had indicated. Somewhere, either up or down the coast, was Colon, the Atlantic terminal of the Panama canal, and to reach that place ought not to be especially difficult, because our small boats were in fairly good condition.

The river made a bend just ahead of us, and my first thought was to get out a boat and explore the stream for a way. We might find some village, I imagined, or at least some evidence of human habitation.

So I ordered the gig lowered and took with me four men, besides Duncan Moit, who wanted to go along and begged the privilege. The current was languid and easy to breast, so we made excellent progress.

Bend after bend we made, for the stream was as crooked as a ram's horn; but always the forest towered on the one hand and the low, marshy flats prevailed upon the other.

Rowing close to the shore, under the shadow of the trees, we could hear the stealthy sound of wild beasts in the wilderness, and once we espied a sleek jaguar lying flat upon the bank to drink. But no sign of man or civilization of any sort did we encounter. Even the woodman's axe was nowhere in evidence.

We hugged the forest for several miles, finding the river easily navigable for small steamers. Then we decided to return, and followed the edge of the opposite marsh, which was much less inviting and less liable to be inhabited than the other shore.

We were scarcely a mile from the ship when Moit suddenly exclaimed:

"Isn't that a canoe?"

"Where?" I asked.

He pointed to a small inlet, and I could see plainly a craft that looked like an Indian dugout lying among the reeds.

"Let us get it and see what it looks like," said I, hailing with some satisfaction this first evidence of human handicraft.

At the word my men rowed in, and the sailor in the bow, as he grasped the gunwale of the canoe, uttered a startled cry.

"What is it?" I asked.

Without reply he drew the canoe alongside our boat, and we could all see the form of a man lying flat upon his face on the rough bottom.

CHAPTER SIX
THE DEAD MAN'S STORY

TURN HIM OVER, Tom," said I, softly, and the sailor clambered into the canoe and obeyed — rather gingerly, though, for no one likes to touch a dead man.

The bearded face and staring eyes that confronted us were those of one of our own race, a white man who had been shot through the heart with an arrow that still projected from the wound. His clothing was threadbare and hung almost in rags, while his feet were protected by rude sandals of bark laced with thongs of some vegetable fibre. He was neither a Mexican nor a Spaniard, but I judged him a North American of German descent, if his physiognomy could be trusted.

The man had not long been dead, that was quite evident, and the arrow that had pierced his heart must have killed him instantly. I pulled out the weapon and found it of skillful construction, — a head of hammered bronze fastened to a shaft most delicately shaped and of a wood that resembled yew. It differed materially from any Indian arrow I had ever before seen.

The mystery of this man's life and death seemed impenetrable, and I ordered the canoe attached to our stern and towed it in our wake down to the ship.

A sailor's burial ground is the sea; so I decided to sew the corpse in sacking, weight it heavily, and sink it in the deepest water of the river.

Before doing this one of the men searched the pockets of the tattered clothing and drew out a small book that looked like a diary, a pocket-knife, several bits of lead-pencil and a roll of thin bark tied with wisps of the same material.

These things I took charge of, and then watched the obsequies. These were quickly performed, Ned reading a short prayer from his Bible by way of ceremony while all our company stood with bared heads. Then the men rowed the body out to the deepest part of the river, and as I watched them from the deck I noticed they were thrown into a state of sudden excitement and heard cries of anger and alarm. Lifting my glass into position I discovered the cause of this. The boat was surrounded by sharks, their dark heads and white bellies alternating as they slowly swam round and round, attracted by the scent of prey. I yelled to the men to bring the body back, but they were too excited to hear me and the next instant had dumped the weighted sack overboard and begun to row back to the wreck at racing speed.

It was just as well, however. I am quite sure the poor fellow reached bottom before a shark could seize him, and once on the bottom they would be unable to either see him or grasp him in their jaws.

Seated on the deck with the others and shaded from the sun by a heavy awning, I glanced at the diary and found that the murdered man had not made a daily record, but had written upon the pages a sort of narrative, which seemed likely to prove interesting. So I asked Duncan Moit to read it aloud, which he did. I have it beside me now, and copy the following word for word as it was first read to us that day in the tropics with the wilderness all around us.

"My name is Maurice Kleppisch," it began, "by profession an engineer and mining expert residing at Denver, Colorado, at those times when I am at home.

"THE ARROW MUST HAVE KILLED HIM INSTANTLY."

"Nine years ago I was sent to the Republic of Colombia to examine a mine, and while there I joined myself to a party that was formed to visit the San Blas Country, at the south of Panama, and trade with the Indians who are the masters of a vast territory there. I am no trader, but my object was to take advantage of this opportunity to investigate the mining possibilities of the wild and unknown region of San Blas, thinking that should I fall in with traces of gold my fortune would be made.

"But, when we arrived at the border, the arrogant Indians would not allow us to enter their country at all, commanding us, with imperious scorn, to stand at a respectful distance and display our wares. The traders obeyed without demur, but I was angry and vengeful, and for a time considered my journey a failure. The Indians, however, exchanged their cocoanuts and sheep-skins — with such other things as their land produced — with great willingness and absolute honesty and fairness, and the traders learned that their given word was held inviolate.

"Nursing my disappointment at being excluded from this mysterious country, I stood sullenly watching the bartering when my attention was aroused by an object that made my heart bound with excitement. It was an immense rough diamond, set in the bronze shaft of a spear borne by Nalig-Nad, the king of the San Blas and the most stalwart, dignified and intelligent Indian I have ever seen.

"I will here explain that the strange race known as the San Blas Indians of Southern Panama is none other than that historic remnant of the Aztec nation which, when Mexico was conquered by the Spaniard, fled through morass and mountains, across plains and rivers until they came to this then unknown wilderness. Here they located and established a new nation which they call Techla. Their territory stretches south of the natural depression of the isthmus from the Atlantic to the Pacific, and contains vast stretches of forests and coastal plains, which they have ever jealously guarded from intrusion. No more did they build beautiful cities and golden temples, for gold they had learned to abhor because the lust for it had brought the white demons upon them in Mexico. The white skinned races were cordially detested as the destroyers of their former nation. By them the Techlas had been driven from the abode bequeathed them by their ancestors.

"The creed of the new nation, therefore, contained two prime articles of faith: Never to mine or trade or employ gold in any form for use or ornament; to hate and oppose every white man that came near them.

"The San Blas people are not truly Indians, as we regard the West Indian and Central American tribes, but are well formed, intelligent and fierce. Their skin is of copper-colored hue and they have a characteristic dress that is peculiar to their nation. They have an established government centering in the king, humane and just laws for the guidance of their tribes, and many racial characteristics. It is said the weaker Aztecs remained in Mexico as slaves of the Spaniards, while the nobles and the most stalwart and powerful individuals, realizing their inability to oppose the usurpers but scorning to become their vassals, fled southward in the manner I have described.

"However true this may be, I found the San Blas—a name given them by the early Spaniards but never acknowledged by themselves—to be well worthy of admiration in all ways except their persistent hatred of the whites. They gave our party cocoanuts and cereals, tortoise-shells, skins of wild beasts that were most skillfully dressed, and a soft quality of lamb's wool, in exchange for knives, glass beads, compasses, colored crayons, mirrors and other inexpensive trinkets.

"When I got my eye upon the king's mammoth diamond I was so amazed that I trembled with eagerness. The gem must have weighed full five hundred carats, and being intent to obtain it for myself I offered my silver watch, a fountain pen, my comb and brushes and a quantity of buttons in exchange for the diamond.

"My very anxiety was the cause of my undoing. My reckless offers aroused the king's suspicions, and when my comrades also saw the diamond they became as anxious as I was, and offered so much for a bit of stone which the king had never considered of any value, that he questioned us closely and learned that the white men esteem these gems even more than they do gold.

"Then the king drew himself up proudly and spoke to his men in their own native dialect, with which we are unfamiliar. Several of the Indians brought to their ruler specimens of the same stones — rough diamonds ranging from the size of a pea upward. These they had doubtless gathered and kept because they were pretty, but Nalig-Nad took them all in his hand and, having pried his own splendid stone from its setting in the spearshaft, he advanced to the edge of the river and cast them all into its depths.

" 'I have told my men,' said he, 'never to gather these pebbles again; nor will we ever trade them to the white men. I class them with the gold, for we are determined not to own anything which will arouse the mad desires of your people.'

"A few of the San Blas, including their king, speak the English language; more of them speak in the Spanish tongue; but their own language, as I have said, is distinct from the dialects of the other Indian tribes and the white men have no opportunity to learn it.

"We were greatly disappointed by the loss of the gems, and when we returned to our camp we talked the matter over and concluded that there must be many diamonds lying exposed upon the surface of the ground in some part of the San Blas territory. Else the Indians would not have been enabled to pick up such choice and extraordinarily large specimens as we had seen.

"I did not like to go away without making an attempt to locate these diamond fields, and seven of the party, adventurous as myself, determined to join in braving the anger of the stern Nalig-Nad. So at night we stole through the north forest and by morning had come to the edge of the fertile plains whereon the San Blas mostly dwell.

"Their country may be divided into three sections: First, the North Forest, bordering on the Panama marshes and the wilderness. Second, a high and broad sweep of coastal plains, formed by eroded drift from the mountains. This section is well watered by numerous streams and the soil is extremely rich and fertile. To the east, by the Atlantic coast, are the cocoanut groves, but most of this fruit is grown upon several islands lying off the coast in the Atlantic. The third division lies south of the plains and consists of a magnificent primeval forest which covers thickly all the slope of the mountains. The climate, especially that of the uplands, is temperate and delightful, and it has been stated that these powerful Indians control the most desirable bit of land in the Western Hemisphere.

"It was in the plain that we determined to search for the diamond fields, and as the Indians had arbitrarily forbidden white men to enter their domain, we stained our faces and arms and chests with walnut juice, and dressed ourselves in imitation of the San Blas people as nearly as we were able. And thus we prowled around for several days, until in a rich valley covered with alluvial deposit I picked up one of the coveted 'pebbles,' and to our great delight we knew that we had stumbled upon the right place.

"An hour later we were surrounded by a band of the San Blas and made prisoners. We relied upon our disguises to protect us, but when they had examined us closely the Indians stripped off our clothing and discovered our white skins. We knew, then, our fate was sealed.

"These people allow negroes to enter their country, and even employ some of them to labor upon their farms. Other Indian tribes of the mountains, who are all hostile to the whites, are permitted to pass through the San Blas territory, and sometimes these mountaineers have with them white slaves, who are treated cruelly and obliged to bear their burdens. But these whites who are the slaves of Indians are the only ones ever tolerated in the country, and a band like our own, entering by stealth to secure treasure, might expect no mercy at the hands of the San Blas.

"Being taken before Nalig-Nad at his own village, he condemned us all to death but one, who was to be sent back to Colombia to tell the fate of those who dared defy the laws of the San Blas. We cast lots, and I drew the fortunate number. My comrades, two of whom were young men of position and wealth in Bogota, were ruthlessly murdered, and I was then escorted to the border and set free.

"I reported the matter to the Colombian authorities, and a company of soldiers was promptly sent by the President to punish the impudent Indians and teach them not to molest the whites in the future. After a long period of waiting a single soldier, who had his ears cut off and was otherwise horribly mutilated, arrived at Bogota to tell of the total extinction of all his fellows and to report that King Nalig-Nad had promised to treat in the same manner any who dared to interfere with his authority. The government decided to let these fierce Indians alone. There were other troubles, nearer home, that needed attention.

"I returned to Denver, but could not get this rich diamond field out of my head. I was a poor man, yet I knew where I might obtain countless treasure — if I dared but make the attempt.

"Finally I decided that I might be able to accomplish alone what a band of white men could never succeed in doing, and having formulated my plans I sailed to Colon and prepared to enter once more the country of the San Blas.

"My idea was admirably simple. The Indians feel so secure that they seldom prowl by night, and in their climate the stars and moon are so brilliant that they illuminate the country almost as well as does the sun by day. By stealthily avoiding all habitations and villages, I had a fair chance to escape observation, and the valley I sought was in an uninhabited part of the plains.

"I took a canoe and a package of provisions, and began my journey by entering the San Maladrino river at the Atlantic mouth. I followed this until the river passed between two high hills, which may be seen in the crude map I have drawn for the benefit of others, should I lose my life in this desperate adventure.

"A stream of which I do not know the name enters the San Maladrino just beyond the hills mentioned, and leads to the southward. It passes through the first forest and is broad and deep. Hiding in the forest the first day, I cautiously paddled my canoe up this stream the next night and passed a portion of the plain until I reached a smaller tributary entering from the left. This tributary flows through the most fertile and most thickly inhabited portion of the Indian lands. At the first junction I turned to the right and paddled along until I could go no further by boat. So, secreting my canoe in some bushes, I walked during the following night to the valley which we had before visited, and which lies in the uplands near to the edge of the great mountain forest. This tangled woodland favored me, for in it I hid securely by day, while at night I searched for diamonds in my valley.

"I found many stones, and some of extraordinary size and beauty, but was greatly retarded in my discoveries by the dimness of the light. The forest shaded the valley part of the time, and only for a brief two hours each night was the light of the moon directly upon the slight depression where I labored.

"And now I have been three weeks hidden in the heart of the San Blas district, and no one has observed me as yet. I have secured almost three quarts of superb diamonds—a fortune so enormous that I am considering a speedy return to civilization. Meantime, I have employed some of my leisure moments in writing this history in my book."

CHAPTER SEVEN
THE FOLLY OF THE WISE

NO ONE HAD interrupted Duncan Moit as he read clearly and slowly the above interesting story, but as he paused at the close of the last paragraph I have recorded we gave some sighs of wonder and admiration and looked at one another curiously to see what impression the "history" was making.

"Go on!" cried Uncle Naboth, eagerly. "That can't be all."

"No," answered the inventor, "it is not all. But it seems to cover the period of the first writing. The other entries are more hurried and more carelessly inscribed."

"Is the map he mentions there?" I asked.

"Yes. It is badly drawn, for an engineer, but sufficiently clear, I imagine, to enable one to follow it with ease."

"Then read on, please."

He obeyed at once.

"Last night, as I approached the forest after my work in the valley, I saw a man's face peering at me from between the trees. The moon shone on it clearly. It was an Indian's face, but in an instant it had disappeared. Greatly startled, I searched the forest with care, but could find no trace of the spy. I may have been deceived, however. Perhaps my nerves are getting unstrung."

Moit turned a leaf.

"Again I have seen a man's face," he read. "This time it was in the center of the valley, among a clump of low bushes. I ran to the forest in a state of excitement; then reproached myself for my folly and came back; but I could find nothing."

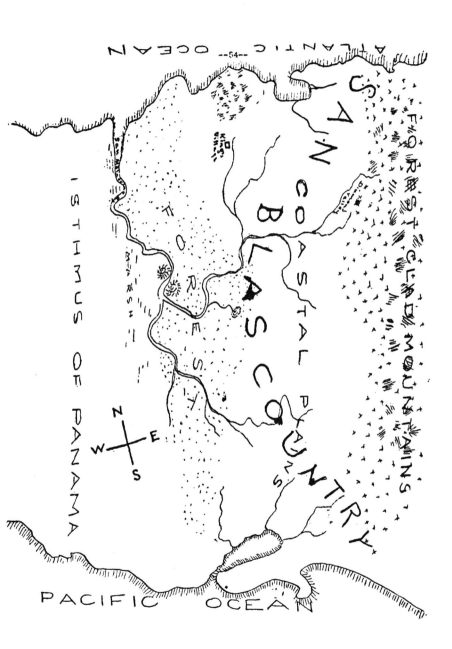

"These are all different entries," remarked the reader, turning another page. "I will read them as they appear."

"I am confident," proceeded the writer, "that I have been discovered at last by the San Blas. They have spies all around me, by day as well as by night, but to my surprise they have not yet molested me in any way. I have determined to get away at once—this very night—but as I may be seized, and perhaps murdered, I shall not take more than a part of my treasure with me. This valley of diamonds is far richer than any field ever discovered in South Africa, and if I am able to escape I shall secure assistance and come here again in spite of the San Blas, So I will leave the greater part of my treasure where it has been hidden, and take only such stones as I can comfortably carry in my pockets. I must write a description of where the diamonds are secreted, for if I am killed and any white man comes upon this book, I bequeathe to him my wealth, provided he is brave enough to take it from the country of the San Blas. Here is my injunction: When you have reached the valley I have marked upon the map, you will find near its center a boulder of deep red granite, bare and solitary, the upper portion bearing an arm-like projection or spike that points directly toward the forest. Follow this line of direction and you will come upon a gigantic mahogany tree standing just at the edge of the forest, which is really a jungle at this point. Back of the mahogany is a large dead stump, surrounded by moss. Lift the moss at the right of the stump and you will come upon a cavity in which I have secreted my hoard of diamonds. You will have no trouble in recognizing the valley, on account of the remarkable boulder of rock, and the rest is easy. . . . I have reached the stream and found my canoe safe; but I must keep hidden among the bushes until another night. I do not think I have been followed, but I cannot be sure. The strange inaction of the San Blas astonishes me and makes me uneasy.

* * * * * *

"The worst has happened, and it is not so very bad, after all. They seized me last evening and took away my diamonds, which they cast into the river with absolute disdain of their value. But then they at once released me, and went away and left me to myself. Fortunately I had hidden ten fine stones in a roll of bark, and these they failed to discover. I am sorry to have lost the others, but these few specimens will prove the truth of my story when I get home. The adventure shows my wisdom in leaving the bulk of the treasure secreted in the forest. . . . There is no use in hiding myself now, for my presence is well known. Why I should have been spared, when every other white intruder has been killed, I cannot explain. But they seem to have made an exception in my favor, and I am jubilant and fearful at the same time. Somehow, I cannot help imagining that these dreadful Indians are playing with me, as a cat does with a mouse. But I shall go boldly forward, and trust to luck to escape."

"Is that all?" I asked, as Duncan Moit paused and closed the book.

"It is all."

"But the rest of the poor fellow's story is as clear as if he had written it," I commented, musingly. "The Indians waited until he had reached the last boundary of their territory, and then put an arrow into his heart. Where he fell they left him, trusting the canoe would float down the stream and warn other whites not to venture too near."

"Do you think that story is true?" enquired Uncle Naboth, with some asperity,

"Why not, Uncle?"

"It sounds fishy, to my notion."

I drew the roll of bark we had taken from the pocket of the dead man and cut with my knife the thongs which bound it together. After removing the outer wrappers I found ten crystal pebbles in the center, which I handed around so that all could examine them with care. Only Uncle Naboth had seen rough diamonds before, but the grunts of the shrewd old trader told me at once that he recognized the value of these stones.

However, I looked up the acid test in one of my books in the stateroom, and was able to apply it in a satisfactory manner. We managed to crumble a portion of one stone and with the dust thus secured Duncan polished a small surface on another. They were diamonds, sure enough, very white in color and seemingly perfect specimens.

And all the while we were thus occupied the four of us were silently thinking. Each one, moreover, took the book and read with care the story for himself. The map was crude enough, but I stared at it so intently that every pencil mark was indelibly impressed upon my brain.

At dinner we were an unsociable party. Afterward we assembled on the deck. Uncle Naboth smoked his pipe instead of the big cigar, but said nothing. Ned put his face between his hands and resting his elbows upon his knees stared fixedly at the deck in meditative silence. Duncan Moit hung over the rail and gazed at the river as it murmured by.

I looked at my comrades and smiled at their absorption. This longing for treasure and sudden wealth is natural enough, and few men are able to escape it. I knew very well that all of us were pondering on a way to get at the diamonds Maurice Kleppisch had left secreted in the forest of San Blas. I may as well acknowledge that I was fully as covetous as the others, but a hearty fear of those strange Indians did much to lessen my desire to visit them.

The evening passed with scarcely a remark, and when we went to bed we were still thinking. Not of the wrecked ship, though, or how we should save the cargo and get ourselves into some civilized port. The reading of the dead man's narrative had turned our thoughts entirely from our own mischance and inoculated us with a feverish desire to plunge into the same adventurous channels that had resulted so fatally in his own case.

At breakfast Uncle Naboth suddenly abandoned all pretense of reserve.

"This is the San Maladrino river," he asserted.

We all nodded, our faces serious and attentive.

"Of course," said I. "He returned the same way he entered the San Blas country, and we found him floating on this very stream."

No one cared to discuss a proposition so very evident, and having hurriedly finished the meal we assembled on deck to resume the conversation.

"Gentlemen," said Moit, "you have all arrived at some conclusion, I am sure. Let us exchange ideas, and discuss their various merits."

I asked Ned Britton to speak first.

"Well," said he, "it wouldn't be right or proper for us to leave them two or three quarts o' diamon's to rust under that stump. I notice the book says these Indians don't have firearms; but we've got a plenty, so I perpose as we march in, pepper 'em good if they show fight, an' then march out agin with the di'monds. I believe if we put up a good front there's enough of us to do the job."

"Especially as a company of carefully drilled soldiers got wiped off the earth," I remarked somewhat sarcastically.

"Colombian sodgers don't count," said Ned. "Our men is the right stuff 'cause they're all Americans."

"I confess that I do not like the looks of this arrow," said Moit, handling cautiously the bronze tipped weapon we had drawn from the dead man's breast. "It is evident they can shoot straight, and there may be thousands of the San Blas to fight, for all we know. I think that open warfare would result in our total extinction."

"If by that you mean we'd be punched full o' holes, I quite agree with you," observed Uncle Naboth. "Diplomacy's the thing; diplomacy an' caution. You can ketch more flies with sugar 'n' you can with vinegar."

"Haven't you a suggestion, Uncle?" I asked.

During several voyages in the company of Naboth Perkins I had learned to have great respect for his shrewdness and judgment, and for that reason I now awaited his reply with genuine interest.

He relighted his pipe, gave two or three energetic puffs, and then began:

"This fellow, you'll notice, tells us a good deal about the San Blas Indians, an' what he says is all worth careful considerin'. They ain't like common savages, but have their laws an' live up to 'em. In one place he says blacks is used by them for slaves, and that white slaves of Injuns that is friendly to 'em, an' not to the whites, is let alone whenever they're in their country. Gentlemen—an' Sam, too—that's my keynote. It tells us plain what to do, an' how to do it!"

He looked at us triumphantly, but I was too stupid to see the point of this argument.

"I'm afraid I don't understand, Uncle," I said.

"Well, you're wrong, Sam. It's a thing you can't help now, but you're likely to outgrow it. Hey there, Nux!" he called. "Get Bry an' both o' you come here."

I started, beginning to see what he meant; but I said nothing until the two Sulus stood before us. Bryonia was tall and slender, and very powerful. Nux was shorter and stouter, but equally strong of muscle. Their faces were intelligent and expressive and their poise exhibited a native dignity. Two more faithful followers no man ever had than this pair of South Sea Indians, and I regarded them more as brothers than servants, for I owed my life to their bravery and care.

"Gentleman," announced Uncle Naboth, "these boys is Indians, and mighty good Indians, too. They're goin' to take us four white folks into the San Blas country as their slaves. They'll be finely welcomed, for they'll pound an' kick us all around, and we'll be meek as Moses till we git our fists on them di'monds. It's jest as easy as rollin' off a log, an' a heap more fun."

I admit the suggestion filled me with admiration, and I saw Duncan Moit's face brighten as soon as he heard it.

"That's it, sir!" he exclaimed. "That is just the idea I was looking for, to connect with my own. By putting the two together I believe we shall succeed without a doubt."

"What is your idea, then?" I asked.

"To travel in my convertible automobile."

"What! Through a wilderness?"

"Along the streams as far as the water will allow, and then over the level plains. The machine will run in any farming country, for you must remember that it does not sink into soft ground as ordinary heavy automobiles do. Indeed, by turning the pumps into the vacuum chambers and exhausting them, I can render the car so light that it will almost skim over a marsh."

"But what's the use of travellin' that way?" asked Uncle Naboth.

"We gain safety, in case of attack; speed, if we are forced to fly; comfort, by carrying our hotel always with us, and, above all, I rely upon the invention to awe the simple Indians and make them look upon us as superior creatures. The machine is here and in working order; it would be folly, when it offers so many advantages, not to use it."

"Very good," said I, approvingly, for I could see the force of his arguments.

"The only thing that worried me," continued Moit, "was the fact that our being white would arouse the enmity of the San Blas, in spite of the wonders we can show them. But if Nux and Bryonia pose as the masters, and we are merely their slaves to run and care for their magic travelling machine, then we need have no special fear."

"Magic travellin' machine is good!" cried my uncle. "You've hit the nail on the head, Mr. Moit, as sure as fate!"

The inventor smiled, as if pleased with the compliment.

"If I can get a share of those diamonds," said he, "I will be independent of my rich uncle in Los Angeles, and will have the means to secure my patents, erect my own factory, and manufacture the machines myself. It is something to work for, is it not?"

I had been carefully examining the proposition, and now said:

"There seems to be a serious flaw in your arrangement, Uncle."

"What's that, Sam?"

"Such a combination would excite the suspicions of the Indians at once, if they are really as clever as they are reported to be. Take your own case, for example, Uncle Naboth. You couldn't look like a slave for a single minute."

Indeed, Mr. Perkins' stout little body, his cheery face and shrewd eyes, and the general air of prosperity and contentment that radiated from his benign personality, were a clear refutation of any suggestion of slavery or even dependence. Even Ned smiled at the idea, and Duncan

Moit shook his head with a sigh.

"Mr. Perkins can't go," he said.

Uncle Naboth looked disappointed, and then puffed his pipe angrily.

"You fellers don't allow for my actin'," he growled. "I'm as good a play actor as ever travelled with a show."

"That may be, Uncle; but you don't look the part, and unfortunately you can't disguise yourself," I said. "But I want it clearly understood that whoever goes on this adventure, we are all to have an equal share in the spoils. For the opportunity belongs to us all alike, and all would be glad to go and do their full share."

"I am willing to agree to that," said Moit.

"Then I propose that you and I alone accompany Bry and Nux on the expedition," I continued. "Two of us are as good as a dozen, for we cannot fight our way, in any event."

"What about me?" asked Britton, anxiously.

"I want you to take a crew in the long boat and try to make Colon, by feeling your way north along the coast. From there you can report by wire our mishap to Mr. Harlan, and get his instructions what to do. Uncle Naboth must in the meantime take charge of the wrecked ship and the remaining men. This country isn't very big, you know; so we all ought to be able to meet again in a few days, when we can decide upon our future movements."

And so the matter was finally arranged, and it was decided that Ned and his crew in the long boat and our party in our "magic travelling machine" would leave the wreck the next morning and proceed in opposite directions upon our respective missions.

CHAPTER EIGHT
THE SAN BLAS COUNTRY

A S SOON AS he was away we began preparations for our own departure. The first thing was to arrange for launching the convertible automobile, which Moit had been examining very carefully ever since daybreak. He reported that it had sustained no damage whatever from the storm or the shock of grounding and was in perfect condition. So all we had to do was to remove the guy ropes, let it slide down the slanting deck to the bulwarks — over which we lifted it with a crane attached to the mizzenmast — and then let the machine descend gently until it rested on the bosom of the river.

I was still so skeptical concerning some of Moit's absurd claims that it would not have surprised me to see the huge car sink like a stone; but instead of that it rode the water like a duck, the wheels half submerged, the rail high above the water-line.

We now filled the ample lockers beneath the seats with provisions, put in a cask of fresh water in case the river water proved unpalatable, and took along such trinkets as we could gather together for trading purposes. We each carried a brace of revolvers, Moit and I (being slaves) concealing ours, while Nux and Bry carried theirs openly.

Finally we dressed for the excursion. The gay checked suit and tourist cap of Uncle Naboth we gave to Nux, and although they hung rather loosely he presented a most startling appearance in them. He swung a brass watch chain of gigantic size across his vest front and Uncle gave him a few of the big cigars to smoke when he wanted to "show off."

Bry wore a white duck suit belonging to Duncan Moit, and to my astonishment looked as aristocratic as any Eastern potentate on his first visit to London. These Sulus were by no means bad looking men and they took great delight in the transformations we thrust upon them.

As for Moit and myself, we hunted among the sailors' cast-off togs for the most disreputable "land clothes" we could find, and those we selected were ragged and dirty enough, in all conscience. I wore a run-down shoe upon one foot and a red leather slipper on the other, and when I had rumpled my hair and soiled my face and hands I am sure I was as disgraceful in appearance as any ragged urchin you ever came across.

I was not wholly satisfied with Duncan, however. In spite of his apparel there was so thoughtful a look in his big gray eyes and so well-bred and composed an expression on his finely molded features that he could not look a servant's part as fully as I did and the best I could hope was that the San Blas people would consider him an unfortunate gentleman in hard luck.

There was much laughter and amusement among the men we left behind on the wreck, when they beheld our queer appearance. Uncle Naboth chuckled until he coughed, and coughed until he choked, badly frightening those who were unaware that this startling exhibition was usual with him whenever he reached that climax of joy which he called being "desp'ritly pleased."

I bade him an affectionate farewell, and then we four got into the "auto-boat." Moit sprung the paddles from the rims of the wheels and started the engines, and a minute later we were waving our hands to those on the wreck and gliding at a good rate of progress up the river.

The bulky machine did not draw so much water as one would imagine, owing to its broad displacement and the lightness of the material employed in its construction. We found the current gentle, and made such good time that at eleven o'clock we passed between the two hills indicated on Maurice Kleppisch's map, a copy of which I had brought with us.

The current was swifter here because the mounds narrowed the river considerably; but Moit gave the engines a little more speed and we went through without abating our rate of progress.

Just beyond the hills we saw a group of Indians standing beneath the trees on the left bank and regarding us earnestly but calmly. Perhaps they had seen small steamers and thought our craft belonged to that class, for they exhibited neither fear nor surprise, merely turning their grave faces toward us and remaining otherwise motionless and silent as we glided by.

I whispered to Bryonia and Nux to stand up and bow a greeting, which they proceeded to do with amusing and exaggerated dignity; and then told Nux to box my ears, which he did so promptly and in so lusty a manner that they rang for several minutes afterward.

I had explained to my blacks at great length our reasons for undertaking this queer adventure, and what we expected them to do to carry out the farce and assist us in securing the treasure. I had even read to them the dead man's diary, from beginning to end, so that they would know as much about the San Blas as we did. They were, as I have said, both clever and resourceful, besides being devoted to me personally; so that I felt justified in relying to a great extent upon their judgment in case of emergency.

Should I need to give them any secret instructions, I could do so in their own language, which they had taught me during the tedium of several long voyages, and which

I prided myself upon speaking fairly well. It was the language of their own island of Tayakoo, for these were not properly Sulus but natives belonging to a distinct tribe of South Sea Islanders which owed allegiance to no other ruler than their own.

Being aware that the king, and some others, of the San Blas knew English and Spanish, I could rely upon this almost unknown dialect to cover any secret instructions I wished to convey to my blacks.

Nux and Bry were not linguists, however, and knew but a few Spanish words besides the imperfect English and their native tongue; but we arranged that they were to command me to interpret in Spanish whenever it was necessary. Duncan Moit, unfortunately, knew nothing but English.

The tributary that entered the river from the left side was a farther distance beyond the hills than the map seemed to indicate; but we came to it presently and began slowly to ascend it in a southerly direction, although it made many twists and turns. We found it easily navigable, with dense forests on either side, and several times we found we were observed by silent groups of Indians on the bank, to all of whom Nux and Bry bowed greetings with tremendous condescension and mock courtesy. The bows were never returned, however, and the Indians stood like statues until we had passed by.

"There is no way of avoiding these people," said Moit, "so I think our best policy will be to go directly to the king's village, which I see marked upon the map, and make friends with him. Bryonia can explain our presence by saying he merely wishes to examine the San Blas country, and when once we have established friendly relations with these natives we can visit several different parts of their territory, to throw them off their guard, and finally reach the valley for which we are bound and secure the diamonds at our leisure."

"That seems to me a capital plan," I agreed, and we decided then and there to follow it as closely as circumstances would allow.

After an hour's cruise through the forest we came to the coastal plains, finding this a remarkably fertile country with fields under fine cultivation. As soon as we discovered a low bank on our left we turned the machine toward the shore, and when the wheels touched bottom they climbed the bank easily and we quickly found ourselves upon dry land.

More Indians were observing us, and as we left the water and glided over the land I detected a look of amazement upon their faces that all their reserve could not control. Indeed, I was myself filled with wonder at the marvelous performances of Duncan Moit's invention, so that small blame attaches to the San Blas if their stoicism could not master their astonishment.

We crossed the plain until we came upon a pretty stream, which we took to be the one indicated upon the map, and from there followed its course eastward, making excellent time over the level meadows. We saw a few huts scattered along the way, and several herds of cattle and sheep, but no horses. The sheep seemed few to supply the wool for which these Indians were famous, but I imagined we would find larger flocks in the uplands.

It was about five o'clock in the afternoon when we sighted a considerable village, which at once we determined must be the place we sought. Bowling along at an increased pace we soon reached the town, but to our surprise we found our way barred by solid files of Indians, all standing with their arrows ready notched in their bowstrings.

"ANY SPEAK ENGLIS'?"

Moit stopped the engines and we came to a halt. Hitherto we had been allowed to go where we pleased since entering this strange land, but it seemed that our license was now at an end.

Bry stood up in his seat, made a bow, and said in a loud voice:

"Any speak Englis'? — America — United States?"

In an instant we were surrounded by the stern-visaged natives, while one of them, a tall, powerful fellow and evidently a chief, stepped close to the machine and answered in a quiet voice:

"I the English speak."

"Very good," said Bry. "I am great chief of Tayakoo. My name is Honorable Bryonia. Here is my brother, also great chief of Tayakoo — he name Senator Nux. We come to visit the chiefs and great king of the San Blas. Then, say to me, oh, Chief, are we welcome? Are we all brothers?"

I thought this was a very good introduction. But the chief glanced at me and at Moit, frowning darkly, and asked:

"Who the white men? What bring them here?"

"You speak about our slaves? Bah! Have my brothers of San Blas, then, no slaves to do their work?"

The chief considered a moment.

"Where you get white slaves?" he questioned, suspiciously.

"Stan' up, Dunc!" said Bry, giving the inventor a vicious kick that made him howl. "Where we get you, heh?"

He kicked him again, quite unnecessarily, I thought, and Moit stood up with a red and angry face and growled:

"Stop that, you fool!"

At this rebellion Nux promptly fetched him a blow behind the knees that sent him tumbling backward upon his seat, and when I laughed — for I could not help it — I got another ear-splitter that made me hold my head and be glad to keep silent. Moit evidently saw the force of our blacks' arguments, for he recovered his wits in time to avoid further blows.

The exhibition had one good effect, anyway; it lulled any suspicions of the chief that the Honorable Bryonia and Senator Nux might not be the masters in our little party. Although Duncan Moit and I constantly encountered looks of bitter hatred, our men were thereafter treated with ample respect and consideration.

"You welcome," said the chief. "I Ogo — Capitan Ogo — green chief. You come to my house."

He turned and marched away, and Moit started the machine and made it crawl after him.

The other natives followed in a grave procession, and so we entered the village and passed up its clean looking streets between rows of simple but comfortable huts to the further end, where we halted at the domicile of the "green chief."

CHAPTER NINE
FACING THE ENEMY

"C APITAN" OGO made an impressive bow in the direction of his mud mansion and then another bow to Nux and Bry.

"Come," he said.

They accepted the invitation and climbed out of the machine.

"Don't be long, Nux," I remarked, in the Tayakoo dialect.

Instantly the chief swung around on his heel.

"What does this mean?" he cried, speaking the same language. "Do you receive orders from your white slaves?"

I stared at him open mouthed, but to my intense admiration neither Nux nor Bryonia exhibited the least surprise.

"Orders?" asked Bry, quietly. "Do you blame us that the whites are fools, and speak like fools? My brother has surely more wisdom than that. If you knew the white dogs, you would believe that their tongues are like the tongues of parrots."

"I know them," answered Ogo, grimly. Then he asked, abruptly: "Where did you learn the language of my people—the ancient speech of the Techlas?"

"It is my own language, the speech of my people of Tayakoo, whose chief I am."

They looked upon each other with evident curiosity, and I examined the two Indians, as they stood side by side, and wondered at their similar characteristics. Bryonia might easily be mistaken for a brother of the San Blas chief, so far as appearances went, and although Nux was of a different build there were many duplicates of him in the silent crowd surrounding us.

"Where is Tayakoo?" asked Ogo.

"Far to the south, in the Pacific Ocean."

"What is the history of your people?"

"I do not know."

"Are there many of you?"

"But a few, inhabiting a small island."

The chief seemed thoughtful; then he turned again.

"Come!" he commanded; and they followed him into his house.

Duncan Moit was clearly puzzled by this conversation, carried on in a language unknown to him.

"What is it all about, Sam?" he enquired, in a low voice.

"The Sulus and the San Blas speak the same language," I replied.

"Anything wrong?"

"No; our chances are better than ever, I guess."

Fifty pair of eyes were staring at us curiously; so we decided not to converse further at present. We stared in turn at the natives, who seemed not to object in the least.

Without question the San Blas were the best looking Indians I have ever seen. They resembled somewhat the best of the North American tribes, but among them was a larger proportion of intelligence and shrewdness. Their faces were frank and honest, their eyes large and expressive and they moved in a self-possessed and staid manner that indicated confidence in their own powers and contempt for all enemies.

Their costumes were exceedingly interesting. Men and women alike wore simple robes of finely woven wool that were shaped somewhat like Greek tunics. The arms of the men were bare; the women had short flowing sleeves; and this was the only perceptible difference in the garb of the two sexes, except that most of the men wore sandals of bark, while the women and children were bare-footed.

The tunic was their sole garment, and reached only to the knees, being belted at the waist. The women, I afterward learned, wove the cloth in their houses, as one of their daily occupations, and the body of the tunic was always white, with colored stripes worked in at the neck and around the bottom.

These colors, which must have been vegetable dyes, were very brilliant in hue, including purple, orange, red, blue and yellow. Black was never used at all, and green was the color reserved for the nobles and the king. I noticed that the chief, Ogo, had a narrow band of green on his robe, which explained his proudly proclaiming himself a "green" or royal chief. The bands of green we found varied in width according to the prominence of their wearers.

One can easily imagine that the appearance of an automobile in this country, isolated as it was from all modern civilization, would be likely to inspire the natives with awe and wonder, if not with actual terror. Yet these queer people seemed merely curious, and tried to repress even their curiosity as much as possible. They knew nothing at all of mechanics, existing in the same simple fashion that their ancestors had done, centuries before, plowing their land with sharpened sticks and using arrows and spears as their only weapons except for the long bronze knives that were so roughly fashioned as to be well-nigh ridiculous. The only way I can explain the stolid demeanor of these Indians is through their characteristic fearlessness and repression, which enabled them to accept any wonderful thing without displaying emotion.

But they were interested, nevertheless. Their eyes roved everywhere about the machine and only we, the accursed whites, were disregarded.

After a half hour or so Nux and Bryonia came out of the house, accompanied by the chief. They had broken bread together and tasted a native liquor, so that they might now depend upon the friendship of their host unless he found that they had deceived him. This was a long stride in the right direction. But when they had asked to see the king they were told that his residence was several miles to the eastward, and that in the morning Ogo would escort them to the royal dwelling and introduce them to the mighty Nalig-Nad.

Meantime Nux and Bry were given plain instructions not to leave this village, and when they were invited to sleep in the chief's house they were able to decline by asserting that they always lived in their magic travelling machine. This excuse had been prearranged by us, for we deemed it best not to separate or to leave the machine while we were in the enemy's country.

As soon as the blacks had re-entered the machine they commanded me, in abusive language, to prepare supper. Duncan at once got out our table, which was a folding contrivance he had arranged to set up in the center of the car, and then I got the alcohol stove from its locker and proceeded to light it.

While I made coffee and set the table with the food we had brought, Nux and Bry lolled on their seats and divided the admiring glances of the surrounding villagers with the (to them) novel preparations I was making for the repast. Then the Sulus sat at the table and I waited upon them with comical deference, Moit being unable to force himself to take part in the farce. Afterward we ate our own suppers and I for one relished it more than I usually did.

In my boyish fashion I regarded it all as a great lark, and enjoyed the humor of the situation.

As it was growing dark I now lighted our lamps while the inventor drew the sections of the glass dome into place and fastened them together.

We could still be observed by those without, for although the top was provided with curtains we did not draw them. But now we were able to converse without being overheard, and Nux and Bry, appearing to be talking with each other, related all that had transpired in the chief's house, while we commented upon it and our good fortune up to the present time.

"After we have visited the king, and made friends with him, we shall be able to go wherever we please," I prophesied; "and then it won't take us long to get the diamonds and make tracks back to the wreck again."

To this all were agreed. Then Duncan remarked, musingly:

"It is strange you two Indian nations, so far removed, speak the same language."

"True 'nough, Mars' Moit," replied Bry. "But I 'spect our folks come from de same country dese San Blas did, an' dat 'counts fo' it."

"This fact ought to help us with them," said I.

"Sure t'ing, Mars' Sam," Nux responded. "Dey knows now we just as good as dey is—an' we know we 's better."

As we were tired with our day's excursion we soon removed the table and spread our blankets upon the roomy floor of the car. Then, with a courtesy we had not anticipated, the crowd of observers melted silently away, and by the time we were ready to put out the lights and draw the curtains we were alone in the village street, where not a sound broke the stillness.

CHAPTER TEN
NALIG-NAD

WE SLEPT NICELY in our rather confined quarters, and at daybreak Bryonia arose and prepared breakfast while the curtains were still drawn. But as soon as he and Nux had cleared away the things we let down the top and appeared in our open car again, to find that the chief had waited so long outside that he was inclined to be in a bad humor.

The rabble did not come near to us this morning, however. Perhaps the chief thought their intent observation undignified, and had ordered them to keep away. But behind Ogo stood ten tall warriors who had been selected as our escort, or body-guard.

When we signified we were ready for the journey these formed a line of march—three in front, three behind, and two on either side. All were armed with stout spears, and each bore a bow and a quiver of bronze-tipped arrows, as well as a knife stuck into his girdle. When we started, the chief brought up the rear of the procession, so that he could keep an eye on us.

Duncan Moit resented the necessity of running his machine at a slow pace, but when he started it at an ordinary walk he soon found that the Indians were accustomed to swing along at a much swifter rate. So he gradually increased our speed, and it was comical to see the solemn visaged warriors trying to keep up with us without running.

Finally, however, they broke into an easy trot, which they maintained for a long time without seeming to tire. I made Moit slow down after a while, for I did not wish to provoke the San Blas at present, and thought it wiser to show them some slight consideration.

The plains we were now crossing were remarkably rich and fertile, and we passed many farms where men were cultivating the soil by dragging sharpened sticks over the surface. In other places were fields of grain ready for the harvest, and Nux questioned the chief and learned that the climate was so uniform the year around that several crops could be grown in rapid succession. They used no beasts of burden, but performed all the labor with their own muscles, which in a measure accounted for their powerful racial physique. There were no roads leading from one place to another, merely paths over the meadows to indicate the lines of travel.

The houses were formed partly of logs and partly of clay baked in the sun. They were simple and somewhat rude in construction, but appeared to be quite clean and comfortable. So far we had seen little evidence of luxury or refinement.

It was nearly noon when we approached a circular enclosure which proved to be a stockade of clay held together with brushwood until the sun had hardened it to brick. There was an arched opening in this wall, and Moit obeyed a signal from Ogo and headed toward it.

Entering the enclosure we found a large, rambling dwelling in the center and a row of smaller houses circling the inner side of the wall. A large space was thus left around the central building, which we naturally concluded to be the king's palace.

The doorways and windows (the latter being unglazed apertures) of the smaller huts were filled with attentive faces of women and children, but not a sound broke the silence to which these natives seemed to be trained. Except on extraordinary occasions the San Blas did not chatter;

they only spoke when they were required to say something of meaning.

The chief directed us to halt before a small door of the palace.

"Get out," he commanded, in the native tongue, "and follow me to the presence of our ruler, the mighty Nalig-Nad."

Bryonia and Nux at once obeyed, but the chief motioned to us to come also. We hesitated, and Bry said:

"One of our slaves must remain in the machine, to care for it. The other may accompany us."

"Both must come!" returned the chief, sternly.

"What! do you give me orders—do you command the Honorable Bryonia, King of Tayakoo?" demanded our black, drawing himself up proudly and frowning upon Ogo.

"The king shall decide," returned the chief. "Come!"

I followed them in and Duncan remained with the machine. We passed through a hallway and came upon a central courtyard, built in the Spanish style. Here, upon a rude bench, sat an old warrior with a deeply lined face and long locks sprinkled with gray. His eyes were large and black and so piercing in their gaze that they seemed to probe one through and through, yet the expression of the man's countenance was just now gentle and unassuming.

He had neither the stern nor the fierce look we had remarked in so many of the San Blas, but one might well hesitate to deceive the owner of that square chin and eagle-like glance.

The king wore a white robe with seven broad stripes of green woven into its texture, and on his knees were seated two children, a curly-headed little maid of about ten years and a calm faced boy of five. His surroundings were exceedingly simple, and the only others present were a group of warriors squatting in a far corner.

"Well, you are here at last," said Nalig-Nad, looking at us over the heads of the children as we ranged ourselves before him and bowed with proper deference. "Which is your leader?"

"My friend, the Senator Nux, and I, the Honorable Bryonia, are alike kings and rulers in our own country," was the reply. "But my friend is modest, and at his request I will speak for us both."

"Good!" ejaculated Nalig-Nad. "Sit down, my brothers; kings must not stand in my presence."

They sat upon a bench, and Nux, thinking this the right time to be impressive, got out a big cigar and lighted it, having offered another to the king, who promptly refused it.

"Why are you here to honor me with your presence?" was the next question, quietly put.

"In our magic travelling machine we are making a trip around the world," began Bryonia, in a bombastic tone. They were speaking in the native dialect, which I clearly understood; and I must say that my men expressed themselves much better in that than they did in English.

The king took a bit of green chalk from his pocket and made a mark upon the bench beside him.

"Where did you get your white slaves?" he enquired.

"They were shipwrecked upon the island which we rule, and we made them our slaves," said Bry.

The king made a second chalk mark.

"And where did you get the magic machine for travelling upon both land and water?" It was evident he had been well informed of our movements.

"It was made for us by a wizard of our island," said Bry.

"What island?"

"Tayakoo."

A third chalk mark.

93

"Does it belong to you?"

"Yes."

Another mark.

"And now," said the king, looking at them curiously, "tell me what request you have to make."

"A request?"

"Yes; you asked to see the King of the San Blas. Then you wish something. I am the King."

Bryonia hesitated.

"We wish to see all things," said he, slowly, "and so we crave permission to visit the different parts of your country, that we may observe what it is like."

"Just as a matter of curiosity?"

"Of course, my brother."

A chalk mark.

"Do you love gold?" asked the king, abruptly.

"No, we do not care for gold."

"Not at all?"

"Not in the least."

The chalk mark again.

"Nor the white pebbles?" looking at them shrewdly.

"We care for no pebbles at all, white or black," asserted Bry, beginning to grow uneasy.

The king made another mark, and then slowly counted them.

"Seven lies!" he announced, shaking his head gravely. "My brother is not honest with me. Otherwise there would be no lies."

Nux put the wrong end of the cigar in his mouth, and begun to splutter and make faces. Bryonia looked at the king, stern and indignant.

"Do you judge us by the whites?" he cried.

"No; I have found that the whites are quick to acknowledge their love of gold."

94

"If you were in my country," said Bry, proudly, "I would not insult my brother king."

"What would you do if I lied to you?" asked Nalig-Nad, quickly.

"You would not lie," declared Bry. "Kings do not lie to each other—unless they are white."

I wanted to yell "bravo!" the retort was so cleverly put. The king seemed pleased, and became thoughtful, stroking the little boy's hair gently while the girl rested her pretty head against his broad bosom.

"The Techlas have reason to hate the whites," he said, with a keen glance at me. "They drove us from our old home, because they wanted to rob us of our gold, which we loved only because it was beautiful. They were cruel and unjust, and lied to us, and had no faith nor honesty. So we fled; but we swore to hate them forever, and to be cruel and unjust to them, in turn, whenever they fell into our hands."

"I do not blame your people," declared Bry, stoutly.

"Tell me, then, why do you of Tayakoo hate them, and make them your slaves?"

"Why?"

"Yes; had you gold?"

"No."

"Nor white pebbles?"

"No."

"Then why do you hate them?"

"Because they are dangerous and wicked. They come in ships to our island and try to make *us* slaves. We fight them and drive them away, but they take some of my people and lash them with whips, and make them work like beasts. Also some of the whites we capture—such as these we now have with us—and then we love to force them to do our bidding. Never has there been friendship between the white men and the men of Tayakoo."

He spoke very earnestly, and I knew he was telling the truth, in the main, for I had heard the same thing before. It was only because Uncle Naboth had saved the lives of these two blacks and been kind to them that they came to love us and to abandon the fierce hatred for the whites that had been a part of their training from youth up.

"I will buy your white slaves," said the king, coolly, "and then you may go where you will in my kingdom."

"We will not part with them. They must work for us and make our machine go."

"If it is magic, it does not need slaves to make it go," observed the king, with a smile.

"Would you deprive your brother kings of their only followers?"

"I will give you as many negroes as you require, in place of them."

"We cannot spare them. These white dogs know our ways, and serve us well."

"Then I will take but one, and leave you the other."

Bry shook his head.

"Whatever else we possess, except our wonderful travelling machine, we will freely give to our brother," said he. "But even Nalig-Nad has no right to demand our slaves, and we shall keep them."

The king seemed disappointed. After a moment's pause,

"Think of it," he said; "and meantime make my home your home. We will talk of these matters again."

He waved his hand in dismissal and turned to caress the children.

Ogo the chief said, sternly: "Come!" but Bry stood still.

"Have we the king's permission to visit his dominions in our machine, while we are his guests?" he asked.

"Not yet," replied Nalig-Nad, with the first touch of

impatience he had shown; "we will talk again before you leave my village."

"That does not sound friendly," retorted Bryonia, frowning.

"Have you done anything to forfeit my friendship?" enquired the king, turning a swift glance upon the speaker. "Be content. Only in the king's village should the brothers and guests of the king remain in peace and comfort. My people shall be your servants, and you may command them as you will; but you must not go outside the wall."

We did not like this, and stood a moment silent.

"Seems to me, King Honorable Bryonia," said Nux, speaking for the first time during the interview and addressing his friend point blank, as if the king's presence was immaterial; "seems to me this new brother, King Nalig-Nad, is not a bad fellow. I like him because he is kind to little children, and I am sorry for him because he is not better informed. But what can you expect, when he stays in this one-horse place and knows nothing of the great world that bows at our feet? If he dares oppose your will, remember how poor and ignorant he is, and forgive him. I know what you are thinking, great King Honorable Bryonia, but I beg you not to destroy Nalig-Nad yet, or to explode his people with the terrible power you possess. Let us be patient. Permit this king to live on, for a short time, anyway. What a shame to ruin this happy home! Be patient, my mighty brother, and soon this foolish Nalig-Nad will have wisdom, and willingly grant all that you desire."

Having delivered himself of this speech, Nux puffed his cigar again and looked at the king with a face expressive of great sympathy and concern.

Both Bry and I were fairly astounded. We had not expected Nux to take part in the discussion, and the pleading tone he had adopted was as good a bit of acting as Bryonia had yet exhibited. It impressed the king even more than Bryonia's dignified assurances, although at first I trembled at the folly of threatening so clever and powerful a man as Nalig-Nad. After all, he was merely a savage, and more liable to suspect us of unknown powers than of unsupported audacity.

We soon discovered that Nux had grasped the situation more clearly than we had. The ruler of the San Blas was used to trickery and cunning and had trained himself to search for hidden reasons in all his dealings with outsiders. The suggestion that the owners of the strange travelling machine, who had so boldly invaded his country, had the intention and power of "exploding" himself and all his people struck him as more reasonable than anything he had yet heard. He was visibly worried, and looked half fearfully at the stern and impassive countenance of the tall South Sea Islander who stood before him.

"We will break bread," he said, with quick decision. "Send away your slave, my brothers, and come with me."

"Go," said Bry, turning to me. "And go you, also, Chief Ogo," he added, imperatively; "we would be alone with the king."

The chief looked uneasily toward Nalig-Nad, who had set the children down and allowed them to run into the house. Noting the look, the king bowed his head to affirm Bry's command. He might with reason fear his strange guests, but he was no coward.

I left the courtyard, followed by Ogo, and returned to where the automobile was standing.

CHAPTER ELEVEN
PRINCESS ILALAH

EANING OVER THE side of the machine, her chin resting upon her hands at the edge of the car, was the most beautiful girl I had ever seen. Her form was tall and slender, her features exquisitely regular in contour and her eyes deep brown and soft as velvet. Her fleecy white tunic was without color save a broad band of green that formed a zigzag pattern around its edge, and in her dark hair was twined a wreath of white blossoms with delicate green leaves.

I noticed that her skin was almost white in the sunshine, the bronze hue being so soft as to be scarcely observable. She had not the same expression of sadness that seemed an inherited characteristic of her people, but gazed upward with a faint smile that showed her dainty white teeth, full at the face of Duncan Moit. When I appeared upon the scene the inventor was sitting on the side of the car opposite the girl and returning her frank regard with a look of wonder and admiration.

A little back stood a silent group of young women, whose demeanor indicated that they were the girl's attendants. Their eyes, I noticed, roved over the strange machine with eager curiosity.

Chief Ogo uttered an exclamation of impatience and strode quickly forward.

"This is no place for you, my Princess!" he said, addressing the girl. "You must retire at once to your rooms."

She turned her head without altering her position and said in a calm, sweet tone:

"Does my lord Ogo command Ilalah, then?"

"When the king is not present it is my duty to guard his women," he returned, brusquely.

With a contemptuous shrug as her only reply she looked toward Duncan again, and as if continuing a conversation already begun, she said to him in soft but awkward English:

"And shall it fly like a bird, too?"

"It can almost fly, but not quite, miss," he answered.

"But it swims like a fish?"

"Yes, miss."

"And runs like a deer?"

"Exactly, miss."

"It would be to please me if it did that," she remarked, very gently.

Duncan was puzzled for a moment; then his face brightened, and he said eagerly:

"If you will get in, I will take you to ride—you and three of your women."

She did not hesitate at all, but turned and called three of the young women by name, who came at once to her side.

Ogo the chief, who could not follow very well the English words, was scowling fiercely, but had kept at a respectful distance since the girl had repulsed him. Enjoying his discomfiture, I promptly opened the door of the car and motioned the princess to enter. She ascended the steps lightly and I pushed her attendants after her, for I scented a lark and wanted to prevent Ogo from interfering.

I could see he was uncertain how to act, and the other bystanders were equally undecided. But no sooner had I jumped in after the women than Moit threw over the lever and started the engines, so promptly that the machine leaped forward with a bound.

100

We circled the king's palace three times, while the dainty princess clung to the back of her seat and laughed delightedly and her women huddled together in abject terror. Every inhabitant flocked to the doors and windows to see us, nor could the natives control their amazement at our rapid flight.

Then Duncan headed for the arched opening in the wall, and ignoring Ogo's wild shout to halt darted through and out upon the plains. The chief instantly notched an arrow, but the princess sprang to her feet and faced him from the rear of the car, so that he dared not shoot for fear of wounding her.

Another moment and we were out of range; and now Duncan, inspired by a natural desire to show his fair passenger what his invention could do, increased the speed until the wind whistled past our ears and our eyes were not quick enough to note the objects we passed.

I own that, being myself a sailor, I was a little frightened at this terrific dash; but Ilalah laughed gleefully and cast a slim brown arm around Duncan's neck to steady herself as she gazed straight ahead and enjoyed to the full the excitement of the wild ride.

There was no real danger, however. The meadows were as smooth as any highway, and in an incredibly short period of time we were almost out of sight of the village.

The thought now came to me that it would not be wise for us to offend Nalig-Nad by carrying our prank too far, so I called to Duncan to return. Rather reluctantly, I imagined, he described a great circle and headed at last for the village, never abating his speed, however, until we had flown through the arch and narrowly escaped knocking over a dozen or so of the throng assembled in the enclosure.

Around the king's palace we again sped, so as not to slacken our pace too abruptly, and then the inventor brought his wonderful machine to a halt in almost the same spot from whence we had started.

We now observed Nalig-Nad standing at the entrance to his dwelling with Nux and Bryonia on either side of him. Now that he stood upright I saw that he towered far above all his people, and was moreover straight as a gun-barrel.

As soon as we halted I opened the door and assisted the frightened attendants to reach the ground. Duncan, how-ever, sprang out and gave his hand to Ilalah, who needed no such support. Her cheeks glowed pink through their rich tinting, her eyes sparkled brightly and there could be no question of her delight in her recent novel experience.

As soon as her feet touched the ground she ran to the king and seized his arm affectionately, crying aloud in her native tongue:

"Oh, my father, it is a miracle! The white man's wagon is alive, and more fleet than an arrow."

"It is not the white man's wagon," said Bry, quickly. "It is our wagon—the wagon of kings—and the white man is a slave whose duty it is to make it go."

"A slave? Oh, I am sorry!" said Ilalah, with disappointment.

"Why?" asked her father, putting an arm around her.

"Because the white man is beautiful as a spirit, and he is good and kind," answered the princess.

I glanced at the unconscious Duncan and nearly laughed outright. That the thin-faced, stooping, dreamy-eyed inventor could by any stretch of the imagination be called beautiful was as strange as it was amusing. But the girl was doubtless in earnest, and being so rarely beautiful herself she ought to be a judge.

The king was plainly annoyed at this frank praise of a hated white. He presented his daughter, with much cere-mony, to Nux and Bryonia, and she touched their foreheads lightly with her finger-tips, and then her own brow, in token of friendship.

"Will your Majesty take a ride in our magic travelling machine?" asked Bry, with proud condescension.

"Not now," said the king, drawing back thoughtfully.

Presently he walked close to the machine and eyed every part of it with great intentness. But it was clear the thing puzzled him, as well it might, and he shook his grizzled head as if he despaired of solving the problem.

Then he escorted the blacks around his village, showing them the various huts and storehouses for fruits and grain; and while they were thus occupied the princess came nearer and leaned again upon the side of the car, Moit and I being seated within it.

"If you are slaves," she said, in a low voice, "I will befriend you. Do not fear, but call on Ilalah if you meet trouble or enemies threaten you."

"Thank you, sweet Princess," replied Duncan. "We may be slaves at present, but soon we shall be free. We fear no danger."

She nodded, brightly, as if the answer reassured her, and walked away to enter the palace, her train of attendants following at a respectful distance.

Ogo and his villagers stood several paces away, silent and motionless. When the king returned with his "noble" guests he noticed the chief and at once dismissed him, telling him to return to his village and be vigilant until the visitors had departed from their dominions.

Ogo promptly departed, but not without a final glance of hatred at the inventor and me. Then the king, with many expressions of friendship, retired into his palace, and Bry and Nux were again permitted to join us.

"Let us put up the top," said I, "so that we may talk without being overheard."

We drew up the sections of the glass dome and fastened them in place, while the natives looked on with renewed curiosity. Then, quite alone although we could see anything that happened around us, we sat at our ease and canvassed the situation.

"If you fellows had been with us," said Moit, "I would have run away with the princess and held her as hostage to secure our safe return to the ship."

"Would you have let her go then?" I enquired, mischievously.

He did not deign to reply.

"We could not abandon Bry and Nux, though," I continued, more seriously, "so there is nothing to regret."

Bry seemed very thoughtful.

"We in bad box, Mars' Sam," he said in his broken English, which contrasted so strongly with the ease with which he expressed himself in his own tongue; "dat king is old fox, sure 'nough, an' won't let us go 'way from here to get de di'monds."

"He seemed to treat you and Nux very politely, I thought."

"All seem, Mars' Sam; no be."

"But isn't he friendly? Didn't he break bread with you?"

"Dat don't 'mount to nuffin, seh. If a friend lie to him, he frien'ship is broke."

"Well, Bry; what then?"

"He know I lie to him."

"What makes you think so?"

"He make de chalk mark."

"But how could he know you were lying?"

"His people see our wreck ship, when we not see dem. Dey see from de trees me cook de breakfas' an' Nux wait on de white folks. Dey see Mars' Dunc put de machine in de ribber, an' we all ride away on it. Ev'yt'ing de king know befo' we come an' lie to him. He know we fin' de body in de canoe, an' bury dead man in ribber. He know dead man wanted di'monds, so he kill him. He think we want di'monds, too; so he kill us if he can."

This was indeed a gloomy prophecy. I had no doubt my man had put the exact truth clearly before us. Our folly in imagining we could so easily deceive these clever Indians was all too evident.

"I noticed that Nalig-Nad seemed suspicious and unbelieving," I remarked, after a period of silence during which we sat staring despondently into one another's faces. "He was telling himself all the time, perhaps, that we were fools, and he had us in his power. Only once was he at all disturbed, and that was when Nux threatened to 'explode' him and his people. He is not quite sure that we cannot do that."

"Nor am I," said Duncan Moit, musingly.

"But they must know about fire-arms, and Maurice Kleppisch wrote in his book that they despised them," I observed.

"Fire-arms do not explode people. I did not refer to them," Moit returned. "But, tell me: if these natives are aware of our imposture, what is the use of keeping up the game? Let us get hold of the girl, make a dash for the diamonds, and then escape the best way we can."

"The girl!" I exclaimed, as if surprised; "why should you want the girl when, as you say, we defy the natives and no hostage will be required?" Moit looked confused.

"She knows the country," he said, after a moment, "and would make a good guide." Then he glanced up at me and added, more honestly: "She's very nice and pretty, Sam."

"She's a darling, old man; I agree with you there. But it strikes me that to capture the princess and run away with her would be to stir up no end of a rumpus. We cannot run the machine through the tangled forests, so the only way to get back is by the river—the same way we came. The king could assemble a thousand warriors to oppose us, and the chances are he'd win out."

"Well, what shall we do?" he asked; "Fight it out?"

"Of course."

"Got to fight, anyhow," remarked Nux, philosophically.

"And we may as well keep up the fable of our being slaves to Nux and Bry," I added. "They may know a good deal by observation, but the chances are they have guessed at a lot; so as long as we pretend to be two black kings and two white slaves they haven't any good excuse for attacking us."

During the afternoon several chiefs arrived at the village, coming in one by one as if from different parts of the country. All had more or less green in their robes, and they were a lot of remarkably shrewd and imposing looking fellows. We decided that they had been summoned by the king to a conference concerning us, for after pausing in the enclosure to take accurate note of our appearance and study the queer machine in which we were seated, they passed on into the royal dwelling.

Toward evening we prepared our supper, while many of the inhabitants came to watch us through our glass case. Presently some one rapped softly upon the glass, and going to the place I saw a woman standing there and holding out a basket made of rushes. I opened a window near and took in the basket.

"Ilalah sends it to the big white slave," said the woman, in her native dialect.

"The big white slave thanks Ilalah and sends her his love in return," I answered, laughing. But she nodded and turned away with a serious countenance, as if the message was no more than she had expected.

I handed the basket to Duncan and gave him the message of the princess. His face lighted up and he blushed like a school-boy, but made no comment.

In the basket were some fresh eggs and a roasted fowl that resembled a pheasant in size and flavor. We cooked the eggs over our alcohol stove and blessed the girl for her thoughtfulness, for her contribution was a grateful addition to our tinned foods.

As darkness came on we lighted our lamps and drew our curtains and after a little further discussion as to our future actions we lay down upon our blankets and prepared to pass a second peaceful night in the heart of the enemy's country.

It must have been about midnight when I was awakened by a strange crackling sound. For a moment I lay still, wondering what it could be; then I sprang up and opened one of the little windows.

Dense smoke was rising all around the automobile, and thrusting out my head I saw a mass of flames underneath us. I drew back quickly, my eyes smarting from the smoke, and closed the orifice.

The interior of the car was now dimly illumined by a dull red glow. Moit was sitting up when I reached out to touch him.

"What is it?" he asked sleepily.

"They have built a great bonfire underneath us," I answered. "Will it be likely to do any damage?"

He shook his head.

"All the harm it could possibly do would be to melt the rubber of the tires, and as they are vulcanized I do not believe any open fire would be powerful enough," he said. "But it may get rather close and warm for us to sleep, so we will move on a bit."

He reached for the lever and the machine started and

107

slowly moved over the blazing logs, bouncing us around somewhat but creating no other discomfort. By raising the curtain in front Duncan could see when we were at a safe distance from the fire, so he stopped about twenty yards away and we prepared to lie down again.

"Some one ought to stand watch," said the inventor; "for if we are sound asleep while they are wide awake they may get into more dangerous mischief than building bonfires."

We cheerfully agreed to so necessary a precaution, and I was glad to find myself selected for the first watch, because by that time I had become as wakeful as an owl. When the others returned to their blankets I settled myself comfortably on a seat and listened intently for the slightest sound that might indicate danger.

Presently I heard another crackling, from which it appeared that our unseen foes had dragged the blazing logs toward us and were making another effort to burn our stout metal car. So I aroused Duncan, and this time we moved around to the other side of the enclosure, halting close to a wing of the king's house. For while the car itself could not burn, a good bed of coals under us would convert it into a frying-pan, and we had no mind to sizzle and brown for the entertainment of the San Blas.

Perhaps it was a fear of setting the royal palace on fire that deterred our enemies from annoying us further; for after this second move we were not molested and my comrades were allowed to finish their sleep in comfort.

CHAPTER TWELVE
WAR IS DECLARED

NEXT MORNING WE made an unpleasant discovery. When we brought the automobile around to the front of the house again we found that during the night the natives had bricked up the entrance arch to a height of some four feet above the ground, using blocks of baked clay cemented together with some preparation that we were not familiar with.

This action was intended to imprison the automobile within the wall and prevent our running out on another excursion, as we had the day before.

At first sight it appeared that the device was successful. A small hut had been torn down to provide the material, and the blocks were thick and hard as rock.

Duncan frowned as he looked at the barrier, and remarked:

"Then it is to be war."

"I knew that last night," said I, "when they tried to smoke us out or burn us up."

"Let us give them a good volley from our revolvers," he suggested, angrily.

"Don' do dat, seh," said Bry, earnestly. "Wait first till dey shoot arrows. We make b'lieve we frien's as long as we can. It gives us time to think what we do."

"Evidently," said I, "the council of chiefs has advised the king to make short work of us. We have probably been condemned already, and all that now holds them in check is their uncertainty of the best way to vanquish us."

"They are a little awed by our wonderful powers, I am sure," declared Moit.

"Quite probable," I replied. "Is there any way to get over that wall, Duncan?"

He did not answer at once, but looked reflectively at the archway.

"We can leave this place tomorrow morning," said he, finally; "but I do not see how we can accomplish the feat before then. Do you imagine we can hold the natives at bay another day?"

"We can try," I said as cheerfully as I could.

But the prospect was not an enticing one, and I began to bitterly regret our folly in ever entering a place wherein we could be so easily imprisoned.

"If we get out," said Nux, "then we mus' fight our way all time. If we bold an' quick, we get away all right."

Nux didn't speak often, but his judgment was pretty good.

"I want those diamonds," I said; "and I'm going to have them. If we go back empty-handed we have made a failure of the expedition."

"To let a lot of ignorant natives triumph over the great-est invention of the century is absurd—it's fairly crimi-nal!" added Moit. "I'm not afraid to tackle the whole San Blas nation in this car."

"Too bad you didn't make it a man-o'-war," said I, with a laugh. "If we had a gattling gun aboard we'd have every-thing our own way."

We raised the curtains, and while Bry openly got the breakfast ready I took careful note of our surroundings.

Some twenty warriors, armed with spears and bows, were in sight, lounging in doorways or leaning silently against the various buildings. They were watching us closely, no doubt; but there was no open attempt to attack us as yet.

After a brief conference we decided not to put down the top again, as the San Blas might take a notion to shoot at any time, and their arrows, while they might not penetrate the netted glass of the dome, might mow us down quickly if we were exposed to them.

But I did not like to acknowledge that we were afraid, either; so I let down the steps and opened the rear door, and Bry and Nux and myself all descended to the ground and grouped ourselves carelessly near the car, leaving Moit alone in the machine.

As soon as we appeared the natives began to come nearer, in a curious observant crowd. Then one who was doubtless a chief came forward and said that the King Nalig-Nad desired his brother kings to attend him at once in his palace.

"In our country," answered Bry, gravely, "it is the custom when kings meet to honor each other in turn. Yesterday we waited upon Nalig-Nad; today he must wait upon us."

"But he is the great King of the Techlas!" protested the other, as if amazed that the command could be disregarded.

"And we are the mighty Kings of Tayakoo, which numbers more people than the leaves of the forest," replied Bry, drawing himself up proudly and frowning upon the other. "Take your master our answer, slave!"

The fellow obeyed; but the king was in no hurry to come.

His daughter arrived, though, fresh and beautiful as a rose in bloom, and the natives made way for her as she pressed through the group.

"A greeting to my friends!" she said in English, and peered into the car in search of Duncan Moit.

"Enter, Princess," said I, holding open the door.

She accepted the invitation frankly, and Duncan took her hand and pressed it to his lips as an old time courtier would have done. She was very sweet and lovely, this Indian maiden, and I did not blame the inventor for worshipping her as he evidently did.

"You cannot today with me run away," she said, laughing and pointing a slender finger at the barricade.

"You are wrong, Ilalah," answered Moit, smiling into her fair face. "When I wish to go, the walls cannot stop me. But we would like to stay another day in your village."

She became serious at this. Thinking someone in the crowd might understand the English language as well as she did, I motioned to Nux and Bry to enter the car, and I followed them and closed the door.

"Listen, then," she said, seeming to be glad of the seclusion. "The king, who is my father, is angry because you have told lies to him. There was a council of the chiefs last night. The white men are to be captured and shot with arrows. The magic machine that is a bird and a fish will be destroyed, and the two black kings may then go free because they speak in our tongue, and are therefore brothers."

"That is pleasant news," said Duncan. "When will they do this?"

"To-day, if they can. I was with them at the council. I told them that I loved you, and would make you the mate of the Princess Ilalah. But to that my father would not agree. He says you must die."

Duncan took her hand and kissed it again, very gratefully and with a look of joy and animation upon his face that fairly transformed it.

"Did not this make you afraid?" I asked the girl, surprised that she seemed to accept her lover's cruel fate so lightly.

"Oh, no," she replied. "For the white Chief I love is

greater than the San Blas. He will save himself and fly, and I will go with him."

"Will you?" cried Duncan, earnestly.

"And why not?" she asked, frankly. "Will the doe leave the stag she has chosen? Could I be happy or content without my white chief?"

"Here is a case of love at first sight, with a vengeance!" I said, greatly amused at the girl's bold declaration. But Moit frowned upon me angrily and his eyes flashed.

"Shut up, you pig!" he growled, and suddenly I felt ashamed of myself for not better appreciating the maiden's brave honesty.

"Is there no way, Ilalah, to make your father wait until to-morrow morning?" he asked, turning again toward the girl.

"Why should he wait?" she returned.

"I have summoned mighty powers to my assistance," declared Moit, after a moment's thought, "and it would please me to await their arrival. It will make me stronger; but I am not afraid if your people begin the war at any time."

"And to-morrow morning?"

"Then, at daybreak, you must come to me, and we will go away and leave your people."

"That is good," she said, joyfully. "I will try to make my father wait, and to-morrow I will give up my power to go with my white chief."

"What is your power, Ilalah?" asked Duncan, puzzled by the expression.

"After my father, I am the ruler of the Techlas, which you call the San Blas. When the king dies, I am queen, with power of life and death over my people. But the king my father hates white men, who may not live if they enter his kingdom, so I must go with my mate to another country where the king does not hate him, or to his own country, where he will rule."

This willing abdication of a throne for the sake of a man whom she had known only for a day aroused my wonder. But I could not fail to admire the girl's courage, and indeed to rule the San Blas was no great privilege, in my estimation.

"If your father makes war to-day," said Duncan, "fly here to me at once. Then, if I escape, we will never more be separated."

She promised readily to do this, and leaving the car rejoined her women and moved away to enter the palace.

I noticed that while she had abandoned all—her life, her prejudices and her kingdom—for her white lover, Duncan Moit had promised nothing in return except that they would not be separated. The thought made me sorry for the poor maid; but it was none of my affair.

Bye and bye the king came out, followed by his chief men and counsellors, in an imposing group.

As he approached, Bry and Nux again descended from the car and stood by the steps, and I followed and took up a position just behind them. Duncan, as before, remained inside. We were all prepared to act quickly in an emergency, but our plan was to secure a truce in some way until another morning. I could not understand why Moit desired the delay so earnestly, but was willing to assist him to obtain it

The king was plainly annoyed at the refusal of the black kings to come into his dwelling. His face still wore its calm expression but his eyes snapped ominously.

"My brothers," said he, "we do not like your white slaves. Years ago the whites wronged the Techlas most cruelly, and the law of our nation is to put all white people to death who enter our country. I am sorry to take away your property, but the slaves must die."

"My brother," answered Bry, "see how much more we love you than you love us. We could kill you in a flash, even where you stand. We could destroy your village and all your people. If we so desired, there would be no more a nation of Techlas on the face of the earth. But we let you live, because we have called you our friend. To break that friendship would be to destroy yourselves. I beg you will not again ask us to give up our slaves to your cruel and unjust vengeance."

It did me much good to watch Nalig-Nad's face. He did not like to risk defying the unknown power of the strangers, but if his own authority was thus ignored he would hereafter be a king only in name. Some of his chiefs were glancing at one another significantly, while others were clearly uneasy at our domineering attitude.

I stood with my hands in the pockets of my jacket and a grin of amusement on my face when the king's roving eyes suddenly observed me. I suppose his forbearance could not withstand the white boy's audacity, for he raised his hand and at the signal a coil of rope shot through the air and a loop settled over my body and clutched me firmly around the chest.

Instantly I was jerked from my feet and dragged into the group of warriors, all of whom, as if the action had been preconcerted, sprang forward with their spears levelled threateningly at Nux and Bry.

CHAPTER THIRTEEN
We Look into Danger's Eyes

THE CAPTURE WAS so sudden that it took me a moment to collect my wits. Although bruised and bumped to some extent I had not been much hurt, and even before I was jerked to my feet I cried aloud to my men:

"Get into the car and watch out! Don't mind me. Take care of yourselves."

They obeyed promptly, but none too soon; for scarcely had they closed the door when a shower of arrows rattled against the dome. All subterfuge and arbitration was now at an end; they had at last "shot the arrow" and we might expect in the future nothing but implacable hatred.

My captors—two stalwart chiefs—having raised me to my feet now held me firmly secured by means of the thong lasso which still encircled my body. The coils pinioned my elbows so closely to my sides that I could not even withdraw my hands from the pockets of my jacket.

They had begun to hurry me toward the king's house when a roar of dismay broke from the group we had just left. I turned half around and saw that the automobile had made a short circle and was plunging straight at the king and his warriors. Some were wise enough to scatter from its path, but the more dignified hesitated and were bowled over like a company of wooden soldiers and tossed in every direction.

The lightness of the machine prevented many serious casualties, however, and while Duncan chased them here and there, managing the huge automobile with consumate skill, the warriors gathered up the stunned and maimed and, dodging the onslaught as nimbly as they could, fled into the palace and houses where the terrible monster could not follow them.

Forgetting for the moment my own unenviable plight, I laughed heartily at the exhibition until the two chiefs pushed me roughly toward a doorway and so along the narrow hall and into the big courtyard.

Here the chiefs began to gather, muttering angrily at their recent discomfiture and casting upon me glances of such malignity that they had the effect of sobering me effectually.

The king came limping in and dropped upon his bench with a brow like a thundercloud. He had not been much injured, but his royal dignity had suffered a severe blow.

While one man held the loose end of my lasso and guarded me, the others all ranged themselves back of the king, who said, with what appeared to me to be unseemly haste:

"What shall be the fate of the white stranger?"

"Death!" they cried, in a fierce chorus.

"And at once," added Nalig-Nad. He glanced around him. "To you, Tetch-Tsa, I allow the privilege."

A stout young fellow with considerable of the royal green in his robe stepped forward with a grim smile and drew his long knife. As I looked at him I clutched with my fingers the handles of the two self-cocking revolvers that were fortunately in my jacket pockets, and which I had been secretly holding when the coil of the lasso settled over me. I was not able to move my arms because of the thong that pressed them against my body, but I pointed the barrel of the right hand weapon as accurately as I could toward my proposed executioner. When he was but a few paces off I blazed away at him.

At the first shot he paused, as if astonished; at the second he threw up his arms and tumbled over.

Instantly I whirled and fired at the man behind, and my position was so awkward and my aim so uncertain that I emptied the chambers of the revolver in quick succession to make sure one bullet would take effect.

He staggered back and released the thong, and even while I loosed the slip-noose I ran toward the hall and made my best speed for the door.

The thong tripped me as it dropped to my feet and I fell just in time to escape a spear that was hurled after me. Another, as I jumped up, slipped past my right ear, and a third slashed my hip. But I fled for dear life and in a jiffy was free of the house and heading across the enclosure toward the automobile.

They saw me coming and opened the door for me to tumble in. A spear crashed into the netted glass just as the door swung into place again, hurled with such force that its point stuck half way into the car and taught us we were not so secure within the dome as we had imagined. But now I lay panting upon the floor while Bryonia emptied a couple of revolvers into the crowd of my pursuers and brought them to an abrupt halt.

"Getting a little warm," remarked Duncan Moit, calmly. "I'm not sure, Sam, whether we can stick out the day or not."

"Glad you escape, Mars' Sam!" said Nux, bending over me. "Bad hurt?"

"I guess not," I answered, still breathing hard.

The black unfastened my clothing, which was saturated with blood just over the left hip. The spear had cut an angry looking gash in the flesh as a passing reminder of what it might do if better aimed, but fortunately the wound was not deep and on account of its location would cause me little trouble beyond a slight stiffness. Nux began to dress it as well as he could by tearing up a shirt for bandages and applying plenty of sticking plaster from the supply we had brought with us. I thought he made a very good job of it, being somewhat skilled in the treatment of flesh wounds myself.

I could imagine how furious the San Blas would be at my escape. They did not venture out into the open space after these two repulses, but hung around the doorways in an alert and vigilant way, being very sure that we could not get out of the enclosure and would be unable to defy them for any length of time.

Duncan rather expected the princess to appear, as she had promised in case of open warfare; but either she did not consider the emergency had yet arisen or she had been prevented from acting as she wished.

"I won't go without her, though," he muttered, decidedly.

"Tell me," said I, "what is your object in wanting to wait until to-morrow before escaping from here? I can't see that another day will bring any better condition to our captivity, and it's a settled fact that we can't get the machine out of this enclosure, in any event."

"Perhaps I ought to explain," he began, and then paused for a long time, as if absorbed in deep thought.

"Take your time, Duncan," I remarked, impatiently.

He did not notice the sarcasm, but my voice aroused him and he said:

"Perhaps you remember that I once told you I used a glycerine explosive of my own invention to prime the engines of this automobile. In starting, a tiny drop is fed into the cylinders to procure the air compression which furnishes the motive power."

"I remember; go ahead."

119

"The feeding chamber is supplied with enough of this explosive to run the machine a year or more," he continued; "but when I made it, in my own laboratory, the apparatus required was so complicated and expensive that I decided to manufacture an extra supply, to use in other machines which I intended to build later."

"I see."

"This reserve supply, in a powerfully concentrated form, I now have with me."

"Oh! Isn't it dangerous, old man?" I asked, glancing around uneasily.

"Properly applied it might blow all Panama to atoms," he returned vaguely. "But it cannot be accidently exploded while it remains in the place I have provided for it."

"Where is that?"

He reached down and removed a square trap in the floor of the car. Leaning over, I discovered a small cylindrical jar, having the capacity of about a quart, which was suspended at one side of the driving shaft. The straps that held it in place allowing it to swing in any direction with the movement of the machine, but any sudden jar was impossible.

"Is it like nitro-glycerine?" I asked, eyeing the cylinder with an involuntary shudder.

"Not at all," replied the inventor, calmly closing the trap again. "It is a much more powerful explosive, in its concentrated form, but may be diluted to any strength desired. The mechanism I have invented for its application renders it perfectly harmless when exploded in atomic quantities in the engines, although ordinary concussion would, as in the case of nitro-glycerine, explode the condensed contents of the extra cylinder."

"I think I now comprehend your idea," said I.

"Yes, it is very simple. Under cover of darkness I propose to bore a hole in that barrier and fill it with my explosive. In the morning I will blow up the wall and in the excitement that follows run the machine through the gap and escape."

"Very good!" I exclaimed, joyfully. "Then all we need do is to keep these Indians at bay until we have an opportunity to do the job."

"Otherwise," said he, musingly, "I would have to throw some of the explosive at the wall, and that attempt might prove as dangerous for us as are the fierce San Blas themselves."

The Indians seemed for some time unwilling to resume the attack. It was the middle of the afternoon before the king sent a messenger from his council chamber to say that all friendship had now ceased and we must consider ourselves completely in his power. If the Senator Nux and the Honorable Bryonia would leave the village alone and on foot, Nalig-Nad would guarantee their safe conduct to the border, and thus they would be permitted to escape. The white men and their devil-machine were alike doomed, and could in no way survive the vengeance of the Techlas. And, unless Nux and Bry abandoned us at once, they must perish with us.

This proposition enabled us to gain the desired respite. Bryonia pretended to consult with Nux and then answered the messenger that they would decide the matter at daybreak the following morning. At that time the final answer of the two kings would be given to Nalig-Nad, and they intimated that they might possibly decide to abandon the miserable whites and save their own skins.

Whether this proposition was satisfactory or not to the king and his council did not appear; but the San Blas evidently decided to wait, for they did not molest us again that day.

As night approached we were somewhat worried lest they should resume the attempts to burn us; but they must have been satisfied of the impossibility of such a proceeding. No bonfires were lighted, which suited our plans admirably.

The moon, however, was brilliant during the first part of the night, and by its rays we could see that watchers were maintained in several places, so we were unable to do more than restrain our impatience as best we might. Moit raised the trap and carefully removed the cylinder that contained the explosive from its suspended position, placing it on the seat beside him. The very sight of the thing filled me with terror, and both Nux and Bry moved as far away from it as possible—as if that would do any good if it went off. But the inventor had handled it so often that he did not fear it as we did, and taking an empty glass bottle that was about as big around as your little finger he unscrewed the cap of the cylinder and calmly filled the bottle from its contents.

I watched him as if entranced, and thought the liquid resembled castor oil in color and consistency. When the bottle was filled Duncan corked it and put it in his inside pocket, afterward replacing the cylinder and strapping it into place.

And now he rummaged in his box of tools and took out a brace and a long bit that was about a half inch in diameter. He also picked out a piece of red chalk and placed that too in his pocket.

We were all ready, now, but had to wait, although the strain began to tell upon our nerves.

Finally the moon passed behind the king's house and sank so low that the building cast a black shadow over the enclosure, throwing both the automobile and the barricaded archway into intense darkness.

"In an hour more day will break," whispered Duncan in an anxious voice. "We must work quickly now, or we are lost."

He started the machine moving so slowly that it merely crept toward the wall. The watchers had doubtless retired, for we heard no sound of movement in the sleeping village.

When we had approached quite near to the barricade Moit softly opened the rear door, left the car, and crawled on hands and knees to the wall. We showed no light at all, and from the automobile I lost sight of our friend altogether.

But presently I could hear the faint sound of the augur as it ground its way into the clay wall. Duncan started at about the middle of the barricade, but bored his hole slanting downward, so that the explosive would run into the cavity without danger of escaping. It did not take him more than a few minutes to complete his task, and before long he was back in the car again, holding the empty bottle before our faces with a smile of satisfaction.

And now the machine crept inch by inch back to its former position, and we were ready for the day to break.

CHAPTER FOURTEEN
We Astonish Our Foes

S
LOWLY THE SUN arose, and as its first rays lighted the cloudless sky Ilalah came gliding from the palace and sprang lightly up the steps that Duncan had let down in order to receive her. Once she was in the car we all breathed easier, and the inventor especially showed his content and exultation.

"Now let them come!" he cried; and each of us felt that the sooner the suspense was over the better we would like it.

King Nalig-Nad gave us plenty of time, though, and we had breakfast while we waited, the princess accepting her share with gracious enjoyment of a meal quite novel in her experience. She was so unaffected and so charming in her manner that already we began to consider her one of us.

At last the king and his chiefs emerged, and we could see by their stern faces that a climax in our adventure had arrived.

Moit was ready for them. He backed the machine around until it was facing the barricade and as far removed from it as the enclosure would allow. He had made Ilalah crouch low on the floor of the car, so that her people would not discover her presence.

A spokesman advanced from the group of warriors and demanded Bryonia's promised answer.

I opened a side window and said, boldly and in a loud voice, that we had played with the San Blas people long enough.

"You annoy us with your foolish demands," I added, "and we cannot bother to remain with you longer. Had you been friendly, we would have favored you; but you are silly children, and so we leave you."

As I finished speaking Duncan opened the window in front of his steering wheel and aimed a shot from his revolver at the red chalk mark on the barricade that marked the location of the explosive. There was no result, so he fired again, and still again.

The natives, at first furious at my insults, now paused to wonder what the big white slave was shooting at, and I saw that the inventor's nervousness or lack of marksmanship was likely soon to plunge us into a deal of trouble. Leaping to his side I pushed him away and took careful aim with my own revolver.

A crash that seemed to rend the very air followed. The machine was hurled backward against the king's palace, from which a rain of mud bricks and bits of wood rattled down upon us, while all the open space of the enclosure was filled with falling debris.

Shrieks of terror and pain followed, while we, who had all been dumped in a heap on the floor of the car, scrambled up and took note of what had happened. The wall had vanished, and only a ragged depression in the earth remained to mark the place where the barricade had lately stood.

None of us was injured, fortunately, and as soon as Duncan had assured himself that Ilalah was alive and unhurt he sprang to the lever and the machine bounded forward and skimmed light as a feather over the littered ground.

I tried to look out and wave an adieu to King Nalig-Nad; but we were off like a shot across the meadows and all I could see was a mass of excited natives rushing here and there in wild confusion.

After fifteen minutes of this terrific speed Moit moderated our pace, for we were miles from the village and pursuit was impossible.

"Where now?" he asked, his voice seeming to indicate that he cared not a rap, since we had managed to escape with the beautiful princess.

"It will be well for us to find that valley of diamonds as soon as possible," said I, "and secure our plunder before the king can raise the alarm and head us off."

"All right; where is it?" he demanded.

I produced the map and pointed out the location of the valley, which appeared to lie in a fork of the river, far to the south.

"We are now somewhere to the east of the king's village," I observed. "The hilly ground ahead of us rises to small mountains between here and the sea; but if we turn south there is open country clear through to the forest-clad mountain range, and when we reach the forest we can follow its edge until we come to the diamond valley."

"That is clear enough," replied Moit, looking over my shoulder.

So we turned south, and presently came to a stream with such steep banks that we could not cross it. The map had not prepared us for this, so we kept to the eastward, endeavoring to find a crossing, until we reached a marsh, and found our wheels sinking into a soft and treacherous bog.

We backed out just in time to avoid serious trouble, and had to go north again, skirting the marsh slowly and with care until we were once more in the hills we had recently left.

This was decidedly annoying, and we appealed to Ilalah.

"Is there not a path from here to the mountains?" I asked.

126

"Oh, yes," she said; "there must be many paths."

"Do you know them?"

"Not to go to them from here. Often I and my women cross to the great forest from our village; but we seldom come here at all."

"I don't blame you," growled Moit. "This part of your country isn't worth photographing. What shall we do now, Sam?"

"I don't like to go back," said I, studying the map with a suspicion that its maker had never been in this section at all. "But we might try these hills. If we could find a path over them it might lead us around the marsh, and then we would be all right."

"How do you know? There may be more marshes," he suggested.

"It may be. This is all guess work, it seems — map and all. But if we reached the ocean we could run along the beach at low tide, and make good time."

"It is certainly worth a trial," he said; "and if we fail we cannot be any worse off than we are at present."

I doubted that the automobile would be much of a hill-climber, because until then I had a notion that the heaviest machines, with the most power to move their weight, could climb the easiest. But a few minutes removed that erratic idea from my mind. We skimmed up the slopes as lightly as an ibex, and went down them much more safely than a heavy machine under the strain of brakes could do. And so, winding around this hill and over that, we kept on at an easy pace until the breath of salt air could be felt and we knew we were close to the sea.

But now the hills became rocky and more difficult. One good sized mound stood right in our way, and after a close inspection of it through our telescope (for Moit seemed to have forgotten nothing in fitting up his automobile) we saw a broad ledge running around its right side which promised a way through to the coast.

By now it was after midday, for much time had been consumed in seeking a path through this wild and unknown country. So we halted for luncheon, and as we ate I said to Ilalah:

"How did you learn to speak such fine English, Princess, when your people have always hated the whites and tried to drive them from your dominions?"

"The king my father," she answered, "is very wise. From his captives he has learned that half of the people of the world speak English. So he thought it would be best for some of the Techlas to speak English too. One day our watchers brought to the king a man and a woman, who were of the English but could speak a little Spanish too. My father promised them life if they would teach us to speak the English tongue. So the man taught the king and his noble chiefs each day in the courtyard of the palace, while the woman taught the foreign tongue to me and my favorite attendants in our own rooms. It was a long task and a hard one, but after many moons some of us could speak and understand the English well enough."

"Did you also learn to read?" Duncan asked.

"No. My father says written words are lies, for when you read the signs you cannot read the speaker's eyes and know that he speaks truth. The Techlas do not love the sign language, and will not have it."

"That is foolish," I said. "If you cannot read, you cannot know what is going on in the world."

"And that is what we do not wish to know," she answered, smiling. "My people say that to hear of other people is to make unhappiness. We live only our own lives; so why should we care what happens in other lives in other countries?"

It struck me there was some sense in that, if their own lives were sufficient to content them.

"What became of the white man and woman who taught you?" asked Duncan.

"After we had learned to speak their tongue my father killed them," she answered simply.

"Then he, too, lied," I said.

"Not so. He promised them life if they would teach us, and they lived. But he could not promise them life for all time, because all life is uncertain."

"So he killed them?"

"Yes; having no longer need for them. They were white, and the Techlas hate all white people."

"Because of their color?"

"Because they once robbed our people and drove them from their homes."

"Listen, Ilalah," said Duncan, earnestly; "the white race that wronged your people was the Spanish race; but there are many whites that are not Spaniards — any more than are all Indians Techlas. So you have no reason to hate us, who are not Spanish and have never wronged you."

"I do not hate you," she answered, taking his hand and pressing it fondly. "I love you."

"But your people do."

She grew serious.

"If I should come to rule my people," was the slow answer, "I would command them to hate and to kill only the Spaniards. But I will never rule them, because I shall go with you to your own country, where you are the king, and help you to rule your subjects."

I laughed at the idea, although the sentiment was so pretty. Duncan frowned at me. He did not tell the Indian maid that he was merely a bankrupt inventor, with no subjects and no wealth aside from the possession of his really wonderful machine. Why should he?

We now moved on again, following the natural ledge of rock that wound around the hill. The precipice beside it grew deeper and more dangerous as we advanced, and the ledge narrowed until often there was barely room for the machine to pass around a projection. Also the ledge sometimes inclined toward the chasm at an awkward angle that forced us to crawl cautiously along and rely upon the rubber tires to keep us from slipping off the rock entirely.

Not knowing from one moment to another what the windings of the ledge were about to disclose, it is obvious that our journey was as interesting as it was exciting. But we kept moving with dogged perseverance until, with the end almost in sight, we were brought to an abrupt halt by the total disappearance of the ledge itself.

With a precipice in front and one at our right, while a steep wall of rock towered at our left, we had no trouble to decide that we must go back by the same nerve-racking path we had come. This was the more embarrassing that we had no room to turn around, and it was no easy task to back the machine over the dangerous places.

Duncan made us all get out and walk. The way he steered the machine along its crab-like course filled me with wonder and admiration, and I am sure Ilalah considered him little less than a god.

We had dropped the dome top to bring the weight closer to the ground, and if the automobile chanced to slip over the edge Duncan would have a good show to leap out and save himself. Yet so dear was the machine to its inventor that I feel positive that Moit, at any time before Ilalah had enslaved him with her sweet face, would have gone to his death in it without hesitation rather than live to see it demolished. But the pretty Indian princess now possessed his heart as the automobile had possessed his brain, and with such a divided allegiance I looked to see him jump in case anything went wrong. But nothing did, and so the occasion to test the strength of his affection for the girl or the machine did not transpire. Knowing so accurately the capabilities of his marvelous invention, he was able to guide it safely until we reached once more the base of the hill and came upon level ground.

Then we all breathed again, and entering the car held a council to discuss our future actions.

"Isn't the Atlantic coast inhabited by your people?" I asked Ilalah.

"Only in the northern part, where the cocoanut groves are," she answered.

Then, as we questioned her, she told us some interesting things about her people. Off the coast were several islands, also inhabited by the San Blas Tribes, the chiefs of which all paid tribute to Nalig-Nad. These tribes hated the whites even more venomously than did the dwellers on the mainland, although they traded constantly with many ships that came to them for their cocoanuts, which are considered the finest grown in all the world.

She said these ships were from many countries, but their crews were never permitted to sleep a night upon the shore and merely landed to make their trades with the natives. The San Blas people built great pyramids of cocoanuts close to the landing places, and when a ship arrived the natives retired and allowed the traders to come ashore and examine and count the supply of cocoanuts. When they had estimated the worth of the offering thus made them by the Indians they placed beside the pyramids such articles as they were willing to exchange, including beads, clothing, tools and liquors. Then they all retired to their ship and allowed the Indians to advance and look over the goods. If they were satisfied it was a fair exchange they took the plunder away and permitted the traders to load the cocoanuts upon their vessel; but if the San Blas considered the offer too little, they left the goods untouched and again retired. Then the traders must add more, until the natives were content, before they undertook to remove a single cocoanut.

No other form of communication ever took place between these two inimical races, and the San Blas island tribes were so rich in cocoanut groves and so shrewd in trading, that they were the most prosperous subjects the king could boast.

Smaller groves were also on the mainland, south of the marsh country, and traders reached that district by entering a bay and the mouths of one or two rivers. But all trading was there conducted in the same manner as upon the islands, and it was only in the north, where we had entered, that the whites came occasionally to trade for skins, tortoise-shell and grains from the farm lands, and with these parties Nalig-Nad personally conducted the trading and was thus able to jealously guard his border from invasion.

I would like to say, at this point in my digression from my story, that many travellers who have had no personal experience with the San Blas Indians have been induced by the unreliable gossip of the traders to write preposterous tales concerning the manners and customs of these interesting natives. As a rule such descriptions are very misleading, and I am quite positive no white men before our visit to the Techlas have ever had the same opportunities to observe their country and their customs as we had.

So much time had been lost in our futile journeying and in discussing our plans with the princess, that the sun was now low in the horizon. It was discouraging to reflect that in all that long day we had accomplished nothing at all since our escape from the village.

To endeavor to cross an unknown country at night would be folly; so there was nothing to do but find a convenient place to camp until morning.

"Our safest plan," I counselled, "is to return to the river the way we came, and paddle upstream as far as possible. Then we can take to the bank and still follow the stream to the valley of diamonds. Our departed friend, the German, was not a success as a map-maker; but we know that he followed the river in the way I propose, so that part of the country is probably depicted on the map with a fair degree of accuracy."

"This plan will oblige us to pass the villages again," objected Moit, "and that will mean a fight."

"Not necessarily. The country is level there, and we can dash by at full speed, before they know we are coming."

It really seemed the only practical thing to do; so we decided to get as near to the king's village as possible without danger of being observed, and then wait until daylight to regain the river.

I kept watch through the telescope as we bowled along over the smooth meadows; and when, just at dusk, I sighted the distant enclosure, we came to a halt.

While Nux and Bry cooked us a good supper the rest of us got out of the car and strolled to the brook to stretch our limbs. I felt that "three was a crowd" and let Duncan and Ilalah walk by themselves. They wandered so far and were so deeply occupied by their own interesting conversation that when the meal was ready I jumped into the machine and ran it over to where they were sitting side by side on the bank of the brook. It was easy enough to do, for I had watched Moit very carefully; but the inventor was not at all pleased with what he called my "infernal meddling," and told me to keep my hands off his property thereafter.

When darkness came on and it was time to sleep I proposed rigging up a little room in the front of the car for Ilalah by suspending blankets from the dome to the floor. In this way the princess would have all the seclusion of a private apartment. But Duncan protested that he had no intention of sleeping while we were in so dangerous a position, and Ilalah very promptly decided to sit up with him and keep him company.

So there was no need for the rest of us to do more than lie down and go to sleep, an undertaking which we accomplished with much satisfaction.

CHAPTER FIFTEEN
WE SEARCH FOR THE VALLEY

A T THE FIRST sign of light we were off, making to the north until we had nearly reached the edge of the wood and then following its curves over the plains toward the west.

In this way we managed to gain a considerable distance northward from the villages, and although we passed some scattered houses and a few groups of farmers who were early in the fields, there was no attempt made to interfere with our progress.

But when we came to the bank of the main river — making the same point where we had first landed — we found a different condition of affairs confronting us. Fully a hundred warriors were gathered on the bank, armed and prepared to receive us. I saw them through our telescope before they could see us, and we halted at once for a conference.

Nalig-Nad had evidently conceived the notion that in order to leave his country we would be forced to pass down the river at this point, and therefore it was here that he had determined to assemble his forces in order to stop us. He was right in his conclusion that we needed the waterway to carry us to our ship, but he was wrong in thinking that we were ready to escape.

The approach to the river was somewhat confined, because the forest was on one side of us and the high-banked stream entered the river on the other side, narrowing the plain whereon we could travel to rather a small space. It would be impossible to proceed without coming into contact with the band of natives ahead of us.

These warriors seemed intent on watching the river, for they had no idea that we had altered our course and would come up behind them. Indeed, we afterward learned that there was a good path around the base of the hills to the eastward, and had we not been so ignorant of the country we need not have turned back at all. But here we were, confronting a grave emergency, and it puzzled us for a time to know what to do.

Duncan solved the difficulty in his own peculiar way.

"Isn't that a house over there?" he asked, pointing to a roof that showed above a small hollow.

"It is sure to be," I answered, and the princess, who was quite at home in this section, said we were right.

Without more ado Duncan ran the machine over to the house, passing a man who stood in a field staring at us. As we drew up at the door of the primitive hut and Moit leaped out of the car, a woman sprang away like a startled deer carrying a child in her arms and screaming lustily, although Ilalah called to her not to be afraid.

Duncan entered the house and quickly returned bearing a bow and a sheaf of arrows in a leathern quiver. His face wore a smile of satisfaction, but as he rejoined us and started the car again I said to him:

"Do you imagine we can shoot better with that outfit than with our revolvers?"

"Yes; one shot will be worth a volley from a regiment," he returned.

I own I was puzzled, but he graciously allowed me to run the car, although at a moderate speed, so that I had little chance to observe his immediate actions. I heard him lift the trap in the door, though, and then, after a period of silence, he touched my arm and told me to stop. We could now observe with the naked eye the group of Indians on the river bank.

"Who can make the best shot with this contrivance?" asked Moit.

I turned around and understood his plan at once. To one of the arrows he had firmly tied the slender glass bottle, and I could see that it had again been filed with the dreadful explosive. "I shoot," said Nux, nodding his head gravely.

Both of the blacks shot splendidly with the bow, I remembered, for it was their native weapon. But Nux was the best marksman of the two.

Duncan handed the arrow and the bow to him and opened a side window.

"When we get a hundred yards away from the river," said he, "shoot the arrow among the San Blas; but try, if you can, to strike one of those trees growing by the bank. Can you shoot so far, and shoot straight?"

Nux nodded confidently, but held the arrow with great caution and was evidently afraid of it.

The machine started again and rolled over the thick turf at a great rate of speed, heading directly toward the river. Soon one of the Indians discovered us, and gave a cry that turned every face in our direction.

"Now!" shouted Moit, without slackening speed.

Nux drew the bow and the arrow sped swiftly on its mission. The aim was good, but the bottle so weighted the shaft that I feared for a moment it would miss the mark. It flew over the heads of the group, in a graceful curve, and struck a root at the very base of the tree.

The explosion was instantaneous. The tree itself flew skyward and the air was filled with earth, wood and Indians. I do not know how many of the San Blas suffered in this catastrophy, but those who were left were thrown into such dire confusion that they fled in all directions and many leaped into the river in an endeavor to escape.

Meantime the machine never abated its speed for an instant, although the ears of all on board were ringing with the shock. We knew that we must take advantage of our opportunity and the confusion of our foes, so on we drove until we reached the low, shelving bank, and the next moment plunged unhesitatingly into the water.

Duncan sprung the paddles on the rims and turned the wheel to guide our course up stream. Before the Indians could recover we were a good distance away and had turned the first bend so that we were hidden from their view.

"Get out the revolvers and stand ready," said Moit. "They will probably follow, and we cannot tell how long the water will be of a sufficient depth to float us."

But the San Blas decided not to give chase. They had ample evidence, by this time, that we were dangerous enemies, and since we had chosen to proceed still farther into their territory instead of trying to leave it, they would have plenty of time to reorganize their forces and determine on the best method to oppose us.

We found the stream navigable for several miles. Then we reached the uplands, and the water began tumbling amongst rocky boulders in a way that made farther progress dangerous. So we took to the land, gaining the left bank with ease and then rolling along in a southerly direction.

And now we had occasion to blame the map-maker again, for instead of the single fork in the stream which he had depicted we found a dozen branches leading down from the mountains and forming a regular network on this part of the plain. Several we forded, losing more and more our sense of location, until finally we came to a high embankment that barred our way and were forced to follow its course up to the forest, which we reached about the middle of the afternoon.

The grandeur of this immense woodland, as we approached its border, both awed and amazed us. The wood we had passed at the north was nothing more than a grove of trees when compared with the grand primeval forest that covered the mountain as far as the eye could reach.

We hardly knew whether to turn to the east or west from this point, and so we asked Ilalah if she had any idea in which direction lay the valley where the "white pebbles" were found.

She had none at all. The law forbidding the Techlas to gather these pebbles was passed by the king her father years ago, when she was but a child. No one had ever mentioned in her hearing where they had been found.

Fairly bewildered as to our whereabouts, by this time, we turned to the left and, easily fording now the shallow streams we encountered, visited several valleys without having a notion whether any of them was the one we sought, or not.

Finally I said to the princess:

"The place we seek has a great rock of red granite stone in the center, and a part of the rock points like an arm directly at the forest."

"Oh, yes!" she exclaimed; "that place I remember well, for I have visited it often as a girl."

Here was cheering news, indeed.

"Is it near here?" asked Duncan.

"It is far to the right," she answered, after some thought. "We should not have come in this direction at all."

Blaming ourselves for our stupidity in not questioning the girl about this land-mark before, we turned the machine again and began to double on our tracks.

"This means spending another night in the wilderness," said Moit; but he spoke with unusual cheerfulness, and I reflected that as long as Ilalah was by his side our inventor was not likely to complain of the length of this trip.

"But there seem to be no Indians in this neighborhood to annoy us," I observed. "Do you know, Duncan, I believe that your invention of the glycerine explosive is almost as important as the machine itself?"

"Oh, it has helped us nicely in two emergencies, so far," he answered soberly; "but I hope we shall not be called upon to use it again. It is so powerful that it frightens me. Every time I handle it I place all of us in as much danger as I do our enemies, for a premature explosion is not unlikely to happen. Especially is this true in so hot a climate as the one we are now travelling in. The can that contains the glyceroid was quite warm when I filled that bottle to-day, and this condition adds to its tendency to explode."

It made me a little uneasy to hear this.

"Doesn't it require a jar to set it off?" I asked.

"Almost always. And there is less chance of a jar to the can if we leave it alone."

We finally reached the place where we had first arrived at the forest, and fording the stream, which was shallow as it came from the wood, continued our search to the westward. The country was very beautiful around here, and when I asked Ilalah why it was not more thickly settled she said that the forest was full of terrible beasts and serpents, which attacked men fearlessly and destroyed them. So few cared to live in the neighborhood.

We were not afraid, though, with the protection of the car, and when the princess recognized, just at dark, a familiar landmark, and assured us the valley we sought was not far distant, we decided to make our camp where we were and await the morning to complete our quest.

The temperature cooled rapidly in the shade of the forest, and we were now in the uplands, too, where the day was never as sultry as on the lower plains; so we thoroughly enjoyed the evening.

Ilalah sang sweetly some of her native songs, and Nux and Bry favored us with a duet that they had learned in their own far away island home. So we were merry enough until bedtime, and then, the Sulus being appointed to keep watch, the rest of us turned in and slept fairly well until morning, despite the sound of an occasional wild beast prowling around our glass-covered retreat.

CHAPTER SIXTEEN
THE ARROW-MAKER

WE WERE UP and stirring early, and after a good breakfast and a draught of cool water from a sparkling brook near by, we started again in search of the valley of diamonds.

An hour's swift run brought us to the slight depression in which stood the great block of red granite we had so eagerly sought. There was no mistaking it, as the German had said; curiously enough, it was the only granite boulder we had seen in this country.

A long, horizontal spike of rock near the apex pointed unerringly into the near-by forest, and I dismounted and walked from the boulder slowly in the direction indicated by the guide.

Sure enough, on reaching the forest I found myself confronting a gigantic mahogany tree, standing a little in advance of its fellows; so with a shout of joy I beckoned to my comrades and waited for them to join me. Duncan ran the automobile close up to the edge of the wood, and then stopped the engines and closed the door of the dome so that we could all take part in the discovery of the diamonds.

Entering the forest, which was quite open and clear at this one spot, we had no difficulty in finding the dead stump, and then I fell upon my knees and began to remove the thick moss that clung to the ground all around the stump.

I was scarcely more excited than the others—if I may except the princess, to whom treasure had no meaning. Moit, Nux and Bry were all bending over me, while in the background the Indian maiden watched us with a plaintive smile. To her this anxiety to secure a collection of pebbles was not quite comprehensible.

At first the moss resisted my efforts. Then, as I moved farther around, a great patch of the growth suddenly gave way to my grasp and disclosed a large cavity between two prongs of the stump.

I leaned over to look. Then I thrust in my arm to make sure.

The cavity was empty.

"Try somewhere else!" cried Moit, hoarsely. He had risked a good deal for the gems which were to enable him to become famous and wealthy, and this disappointment was sufficient to fill his heart with despair, had he not found another treasure in Ilalah which might somewhat mitigate this baffling failure.

I worked all around the stump, digging up the moss with my knife and finger-nails; but in every other place the ground was solid. There was but this one vacant cavity, and when at last we knew the truth we stared at each other in absolute dejection.

"He must have put them there, though," I said, hopelessly. "The trouble is that someone else has taken them away."

"Oh, yes; I did it," said a strange voice at our side.

I turned and found a tiny Indian standing near us. At first I thought it was a child, but looking more closely perceived the lines of age on his thin face and streaks of gray in his hair. Yet so small was his stature that he was no taller than my breast.

He wore the ordinary San Blas tunic, striped with purple and yellow, a narrow band of green showing between the two plebeian colors. When first we saw him he had assumed a dignified pose and with folded arms was looking upon us with a calm and thoughtful countenance.

"Greetings, Tcharn!" exclaimed the princess, in a pleased and kindly tone.

The dwarf, or liliputian, or whatever he might be, advanced to her with marked but somewhat timid respect and touched the fingers of his right hand to the fair brow she bent toward him. Then he retreated a pace and laid his hand upon his heart.

"My Princess is welcome to my forest," he said in his native tongue.

"Is it near here, then, that you live, my Tcharn?" she enquired.

"Very near, my Princess."

"But tell us," I cried, unable to control myself longer, "did you find many of the white pebbles in this cavity, and did you take them all away?"

"Yes," he answered readily, with a nod of his small head; "I found them and I took them away, and they were many."

"But why did you take them?" asked the girl, who, without knowing the value to us of the stones, was able to sympathize with us in our bitter disappointment.

Tcharn was thoughtful. He sat upon the stump and for a moment studied the various faces turned toward him.

"Some time ago," said he, "a white man came to this valley, which our laws forbid the whites to enter. Perhaps he did not know that I rule the forest which is my home — that I am the Master Workman of the Techla nation. Why should he know that? But the white beast was well aware that his race is by us hated and detested" — here he cast a sinister glance at Duncan and myself — "and barred from our domain. He sneaked in like a jackal, hiding himself by day while by night he prowled around upon all fours, gathering from off the ground the pebbles which our master the king has forbidden any man to see or to touch.

144

"Day after day I watched the white man at his unlawful toil. I sent tidings to Nalig-Nad, the king, who laughed at the cowardly intruder, and bade me continue to watch and to notify him if the beast tried to escape.

"Finally he saw my face among the trees, and it frightened him. He prepared to run away, and buried all the pebbles he had found under the moss beside this stump. Then he slunk from the valley and I let him go; for the king had been notified and would look after him."

This relation proved to us the honesty of the German's story. We knew well the rest of the tragic tale, and were just then more deeply interested in the loss of the diamonds.

"Why did you dig up the pebbles, when the commands of your king forbade you to touch them?" I asked, in a bitter tone.

The little Indian gave me a scornful look and said to Ilalah:

"Must I answer the white child, my Princess?"

"It will please me to have you do so," she answered. "I must tell you, Tcharn, that these white people are my friends. Those who love me will also befriend them, and treat them kindly."

For a time the dwarf stood motionless, frowning and staring stolidly upon the ground. Then he looked up and said:

"Does Nalig-Nad also love these whites?"

"He hates them, and seeks their destruction," Ilalah replied.

The dwarf smiled.

"Then they will be destroyed," he prophesied.

"Not so, my Tcharn," replied the princess, gently. "The power of these white chieftains is greater than the power of Nalig-Nad."

Tcharn grew thoughtful again.

"I saw them approach in a moving house, that seemed alive and yet was not," he remarked.

"That is but one proof of their might," said she.

"And is my Princess now opposed to her father the King?"

"Yes, Tcharn, in this one thing."

"Then," said he, "I will stand by your side, for my blood is the blood of your dead mother, and not the blood of Nalig-Nad."

"But the pebbles!" I cried, impatiently. "Tell us what you have done with them."

He turned his sombre eyes in my direction.

"I carried the pebbles to my own dwelling," he returned. "They are beautiful, and when the sun kisses them they borrow its light and glow like fireflies at dusk. I love the pebbles; so I took them, and they are mine."

This was exasperating to a degree.

"You had no right to do that," I protested. "Your king has forbidden you to gather the pebbles."

"I did not gather them; I but took them from the place where the white jackal had placed them."

"The king will punish you for keeping them!"

"The king? Ah, the king will not know. And we are opposed to the king just now, the Princess Ilalah and myself," with a queer smile. "But you are strangers, and therefore you do not know that in my forest even Nalig-Nad dare not molest the Master Workman."

The last words were spoken confidently, and his prompt defiance of the king pleased me.

"Who is this man, Ilalah?" asked Duncan.

"Tcharn is my mother's cousin," she replied, with frankness, "and in my mother's veins flowed the most royal blood of our great ancestors. For this reason Tcharn is a person of consequence among my people. He is called the Arrow-Maker, and forges all the arrow-heads that the Techlas use. No one else is allowed to work in metals, which Tcharn brings from the mountains. In this forest—I do not know exactly where—is his secret work-shop and his dwelling place. Only one thing is forbidden him, under penalty of torture and death: to gather or use the loathsome gold which was at one time the curse of the Techlas. In all else Tcharn is master of the forest, and the people honor and avoid him."

An important individual, truly, and one who doubtless realized his own importance. Since he had secured the diamonds and loved their beauty it would be difficult to wrest them from him.

While the princess had spoken the little Techla had been regarding her with an uneasy look.

"I see trouble in Ilalah's path," he now remarked gravely.

"Am I not the princess?" she asked, proudly.

"You are the princess, and one day you will succeed your father as ruler of the Techlas—if you live. If you do not live, Nalig-Nad's children by another mother will succeed him. Will you live, Ilalah—you who defy the traditional hatred of your race for the cursed white people?"

Ilalah flushed a little, but not with fear. She wanted Tcharn to understand her, though, and began to tell him how the white people had for many ages dominated the world beyond the seas, where they had many distinct nations that warred with each other. Some of the white nations were strong, and just, and wise; others were strong, but wicked and unjust. It was one of these latter nations, she explained, whose people were known as Spaniards, that had invaded the country of her forefathers and robbed and oppressed them; therefore the Techlas, knowing no better, had hated all of the white nations instead of that especial one that had wronged them.

"These friends," she added, pointing to us, "have never injured us, nor have their people, who have themselves warred with the Spaniards, our old and hated enemies. Why then, should I condemn and hate the innocent?"

The dwarf listened carefully to this explanation, and without answering her appeal he said, in a doubtful tone:

"The chiefs who rule the islands and the coast, all of whom trade with the whites, have told me they are all alike. They are never satisfied, but always want something that belongs to others." I laughed at his shrewd observation, for that was our case, just then. We wanted the diamonds.

"Will you not permit us to see the beautiful pebbles?" I asked. Tcharn hesitated.

"Will you let me see your moving house?" he demanded.

I nearly yelled with delight. I had been searching my brain for some way to win this strange personage to our side, and he promptly put himself in our hands by acknowledging his curiosity concerning our machine. But this proved his intelligence, too, and betrayed his mechanical instinct, so that it increased our respect for him.

"We will explain to you our moving house, which is the most wonderful thing ever made by the hands of man," I answered, seriously, "and we will also take you to ride in it, that you may know how and why it moves. But in return you must take us to your dwelling and show us the pebbles."

I was rather surprised that he consented readily.

"It is a bargain," said he, quietly, and Ilalah whispered that his word might be depended upon.

So we all walked out of the forest to where we had left

the car, which Tcharn first examined from the outside with minute intentness.

"Here is a man who might steal my patents, if he lived in our world," remarked the inventor, with a smile. But as there was no danger to be apprehended Moit took pains to explain to the dwarf how the machine would float and move in the water as well as travel upon the land, and then he took the little Indian inside and showed him all the complicated mechanism and the arrangements for promoting the comfort and convenience of the passengers.

Tcharn listened with absorbed interest, and if he failed to comprehend some of the technical terms — which is very probable, as I was obliged to translate most of the description and there were no words in the native language to express mechanical terms — he allowed neither word nor look to indicate the fact.

Afterward Moit started the car and gave the arrow-maker an impressive ride around the valley, gradually increasing the speed until we very nearly flew over the ground.

When, at last, we came to a halt at the forest's edge, it was evident we had won the dwarf completely. His face was full of animation and delight, and he proceeded to touch each of our foreheads, and then his own heart, to indicate that we were henceforth friends.

"We will ride into the forest," he said. "I will show you the way."

It suited us very well to hide the machine among the trees, for we might expect the natives to search for us and give us further annoyance. But we failed to understand how the big machine might be guided into the tangled forest.

Tcharn, however, knew intimately every tree and shrub. He directed Moit to a place where we passed between two giant mahoganies, after which a sharp turn disclosed an avenue which led in devious windings quite a distance into the wood. Sometimes we barely grazed a tree-trunk on either side or tore away a mass of clinging vines or dodged, by a hair's breadth, a jagged stump; and, after all, our journey was not a great way from the edge of the forest and we were soon compelled to halt for lack of a roadway.

"The rest of the distance we will walk," announced the dwarf. "Follow me, if you will."

I shall never forget the impressiveness of this magnificent forest. The world and its glaring sunlight were shut out. Around our feet was a rank growth of matted vines, delicate ferns and splendid mosses. We stood in shadow-land, a kingdom of mystery and silence. The foliage was of such dainty tracery that only in the deep seas can its equal be found, and wonderful butterflies winged their way between the tender plants, looking like dim ghosts of their gorgeous fellows in the outer world. Here was a vast colonade, the straight, slender, gray tree-trunks supporting a massive roof of green whose outer branches alone greeted the sun. Festooned from the upright columns were tangled draperies of climbing vines which here rested in deep shadow and there glowed with a stray beam of brilliant sunshine that slyly crept through the roof. And ever, as we pressed on, new beauties and transformations were disclosed in the forest's mysterious depths, until the conviction that here must be the favorite retreat of elfins and fays was dreamily impressed upon our awed minds.

But almost before we were aware of it we came to a clearing, a circular place in the wood where great trees shot their branches into the sky and struggled to bridge the intervening space with their foliage. The vain attempt left a patch of clear sky visible, although the entire enclosure was more than half roofed with leaves.

Instead of mosses and vines, a grassy sward carpeted the place, and now we came upon visible evidence that we had reached the abode of the little arrow-maker.

On one side was a rude forge, built of clay, and supporting a bellows. In a basket beside the forge were hundreds of arrow-points most cleverly fashioned of bronze, while heaps of fagots and bars of metal showed that the dwarf's daily occupation was seldom neglected.

The tools strewn about interested me greatly, for many were evidently of American or European make; but Tcharn explained this by saying that his people often traded their cocoanuts and skins for tools and cutlery, and at these times he was allowed to select from the store such things as he required.

"But where do you live?" asked Moit; "and where are the pebbles?"

"Come," said the arrow-maker, briefly, and led us across the glade and through a little avenue where there was a well trodden path.

A moment later a mass of interwoven boughs covered with vines confronted us, and stooping our heads we passed through a low archway into wonderland.

CHAPTER SEVENTEEN
A WOODLAND WONDERLAND

WHAT WE SAW was a circular chamber formed of tree-trunks at the sides and roofed with masses of green leaves. The central trees had been cleared away by some means, for a large mahogany stump was used for a table and its beautifully polished surface proclaimed that it had been a live tree when sawed through. Also there were several seats formed from stumps in various parts of the room, and one or two benches and a couch had been manufactured very cleverly from polished mahogany wood.

But these were by no means the chief wonder of the place. The walls were thickly covered with climbing vines, which reached in graceful festoons to the overhanging central boughs; but these were all the creation of man rather than of nature, for they were formed from virgin gold.

Also the ornaments scattered about the place, the mountings of the furniture, swinging lamps and tabourettes, all were of gold, and never have I beheld the equal of their exquisite workmanship or unique designing. The tracery of every leaf of the golden bower imitated accurately nature itself, the veins and stems being so perfect as to cause one to marvel. Not only had a vast amount of pure gold been used in this work, but years must have been consumed in its execution.

"Oh, Tcharn!" cried Ilalah, in a shocked tone, as soon as she had recovered from the wonder of her first look; "you have broken the law!"

"It is true," answered the arrow-maker, calmly.

152

"Why did you do it?" she asked.

"The yellow metal is very beautiful," said he, looking upon the golden bower with loving eyes; "and it is soft, and easy to work into many pretty forms. Years ago, when I began to gather the metal for my arrows and spears, I found in our mountains much of the forbidden gold, and it cried out to me to take it and love it, and I could not resist. So I brought it here, where no white man could ever see it and where not even your father was likely to come and charge me with my crime. My princess, you and your friends are the first to know my secret, and it is safe in your care because you are yourself breaking the law and defying the king."

"In what way?" asked Ilalah.

"In seeking the pebbles that are denied our people, and in befriending the whites who have been condemned by us for centuries."

She was silent for a moment. Then she said, bravely:

"Tcharn, such laws are unjust. I will break them because they are my father's laws and not my own. When I come to rule my people I will make other laws that are more reasonable—and then I will forgive you for your gold-work."

"Oh, Ilalah!" exclaimed Moit; "how can you rule these Indians when you have promised to come with me, and be my queen?"

She drew her hand across her eyes as if bewildered, and then smiled sweetly into her lover's face.

"How easy it is to forget," she said, "when one has always been accustomed to a certain life. I will go with you, and I will never rule my people."

"You are wrong, my princess," declared the dwarf, eagerly. "What to you is the white man's land? You will rule us indeed, and that in a brief space of time!"

"No, my friend," she said, "the house that moves will carry me away with my white chief, and in a new land I will help him to rule his own people."

The arrow-maker looked at her with a dreamy, prophetic expression upon his wizened features.

"Man knows little," said he, "but the Serpent of Wisdom knows much. In my forest the serpent dwells, and it has told me secrets of the days to come. Soon you will be the Queen of the Techlas, and the White Chief will be but your slave. I see you ruling wisely and with justice, as you have promised, but still upholding the traditions of your race. You will never leave the San Blas country, my Ilalah."

She laughed, brightly.

"Are you then a seer, my cousin?" she asked.

The dwarf started, as if suddenly awakened, and his eyes lost their speculative gaze.

"Sometimes the vision comes to me," he said; "how or why I know not. But always I see truly."

Duncan Moit did not understand this dialogue, which had been conducted in the native tongue. He had been examining, with the appreciation of a skilled workman, the beautiful creations of the Indian goldsmith. But now our uneasy looks and the significant glances of Nux and Bryonia attracted his attention, and he turned to ask an explanation.

The princess evaded the subject, saying lightly that the dwarf had been trying to excuse himself for breaking the law and employing the forbidden gold in his decorations. I turned to Tcharn and again demanded:

"Show us the pebbles."

At once he drew a basket woven of rushes from beneath a bench and turned out its contents on the top of the great table. A heap of stones was disclosed, the appear-

"DIAMONDS! THEY ARE MAGNIFICENT!"

ance of which at first disappointed me. They were of many shapes and sizes and had surfaces resembling ground glass. In the semi gloom of the bower and amid the shining gold tracery of its ornamentation the "pebbles" seemed uninteresting enough.

But Moit pounced upon the treasure with exclamations of wonder, examining them eagerly. Either the German or the arrow-maker had chipped some of them in places, and then the clear, sparkling brilliancy of the diamonds was fully demonstrated.

"They are magnificent!" cried the inventor. "I have never seen gems so pure in color or of such remarkable size and perfect form."

I compared them mentally with the stones I had found in the roll of bark taken from the dead man's pocket, and decided that these were indeed in no way inferior.

The dwarf opened a golden cabinet and brought us three more diamonds. These had been cut into facets and polished, and were amazingly brilliant. I am sure Tcharn had never seen the usual method of diamond-cutting, and perhaps knew nothing of the esteem in which civilized nations held these superb pebbles of pure carbon; so it is remarkable that he had intuitively found the only means of exhibiting the full beauty of the stones.

"Will you give me these, my cousin?" asked the princess.

For answer he swept them all into the basket and placed it in her hands. She turned and with a pleased smile gave the treasure to Moit.

"At last," said I, with a sigh of relief, "we have accomplished the object of our adventure."

"At last," said Duncan, "I have enough money to patent my inventions and to give the machine to the world in all its perfection!"

"But we mus' get out o' here, Mars' Sam," observed Bry, gravely.

"That is true," I replied. "And I hope, now that we have no further reason for staying, that we shall have little difficulty in passing the lines of our enemies."

We confided to the arrow-maker a portion of our adventures, and told him how Nalig-Nad had seemed determined to destroy us. When the relation was finished I asked:

"Will you advise us how we can best regain our ship without meeting the king's warriors?"

He considered the matter with great earnestness. Then he enquired:

"Will your machine run safely in the waters of the ocean?"

I repeated the question to Moit.

"Yes," he answered, "if the water is not too rough."

"Then it will be best for you to go east until you come to the coast of the Atlantic," said Tcharn. "The tribes of the south-east will not oppose you if the Princess Ilalah and I are with you. When you get to the ocean you may travel in the water to your river, and so reach your ship."

This advice was so good that we at once adopted the suggestion.

The arrow-maker now clapped his hands, and to our surprise three tall natives entered the bower and bowed to him. He ordered them to bring refreshments, and they at once turned and disappeared.

"Who are these men?" I asked.

"They are my assistants, who help me to forge the arrows and the spears," he replied. "The king always allows me three men, and their tongues are cut out so that they cannot tell to others the secrets of my art." That explained why he was able to devote so much time to the execution of his gold-work.

The servants shortly returned bearing golden dishes of exquisite shapes, on the polished surfaces of which familiar scenes in the lives of the San Blas were cleverly engraved.

We were given fresh milk, a kind of hominy boiled and spiced, slices of cold mutton and several sorts of fruits, including cocoanut meats.

Sitting around the splendid table, which would have conferred distinction upon a king's palace, we made a hasty but satisfying meal and then prepared to return to the automobile.

I think the little arrow-maker was as eager to ride in the wonderful machine as to guide us on our way; but we were very glad to have him with us, and he sat quietly absorbed by the side of Duncan Moit and watched the inventor direct the course of his automobile over the difficult pathway between the trees.

We reached level ground without accident and then, turning to the left, increased our speed and travelled rapidly over the now familiar plains in the direction of the sea.

We followed the edge of the forest as well as we could, for here in the uplands the numerous streams were less difficult to cross; but soon after we had passed beyond the point of our first excursion in this direction we came upon a good sized river sweeping out from the wood, which Tcharn told us flowed into the Atlantic further toward the north. There were dangerous rapids in it, however, so we decided it would be safer to continue on to the coast than to trust ourselves to this treacherous current.

And now we soon began to pass the cocoanut groves, while groups of natives paused to stare at us wonderingly. But we made no halt, for the plains were smooth and easy to travel upon and the less we had to do with the natives the better we were off.

A mile inland from the ocean, the dwarf told us, were many villages. We decided to rush past these quickly to avoid being stopped, and Tcharn agreed that it would be wise. Explanations would be sure to delay us, even if these tribes had not already been warned by messengers from Nalig-Nad to capture us if we came their way. So when we reached the villages we shot by them like a flash, and the sensation we created was laughable.

Men, women and children—even the dogs—rushed from the path of the dreadful flying monster in a panic of fear, and we heard their screams and wild cries long after the houses had been left far behind. These tribes may be just as brave as the ones farther north, but their natures are not so stolid and self-possessed.

The ocean came into view suddenly, and we found the banks so high above the beach that we were obliged to turn north until we reached a small river, the water of which was deep enough to float us out to sea.

Here we bade farewell, with much regret, to our arrow-maker, and Duncan generously presented him with such wrenches and other tools as could be spared from his outfit. These presents gave the dwarf much delight, and for my part I was so grateful for his assistance that I gave him my silver watch, and showed him how to tell the time of day by following the movements of its hands. He understood it very quickly and I knew that he would obtain much pleasure from its possession.

It was little enough, indeed, for the transfer of the diamonds, which were worth a fortune; but the gems were valueless to him, even had he been able to own them without the risk of forfeiting his life.

We left the arrow-maker earnestly watching us from the bank as we paddled swiftly down the stream; but soon our attention was directed to other matters and we forgot him.

When we reached the ocean we headed out boldly, but the long waves rolled pretty high for us, we soon found. It was not at all a rough sea, yet Moit was forced to acknowledge that his invention was not intended for ocean travel. After we had tossed about for a time we went ashore, finding to our joy that the beach was broad and sandy, and the tide was out.

This was the best luck that could possibly have happened to us, and we sped along the sands at a fine rate of speed, resolved to make the most of our opportunities.

Just before we reached the northern forest, however, we found that king Nalig-Nad had been thoughtful enough to anticipate the possibility of our coming this way and had sent a large force to oppose us. They were crowded thickly upon the beach and we were given the choice of meeting them or driving into the ocean again.

I rather favored the latter course, but Duncan's face was set and stern, and I saw that he was intent on running them down.

He increased our rate of speed until we were fairly flying, and a moment more we bumped into the solid ranks of the Indians and sent them tumbling in every direction — not so much on account of the machine's weight as its velocity.

Those who were not knocked over made haste to get out of our way, and in a few seconds they were all behind us and we could slacken our terrible pace with safety.

We had passed the mouths of several streams on our way, and circled some remarkably broad and pretty bays, so now we began to look for the river in which our wrecked ship was stranded. One broad inlet we paddled up for a way, but it led straight into the wood; so we backed out again, and the next time were more successful;

for soon we were able to discern the *Gladys H.* lying on her side, and knew we were near our journey's end.

Ilalah told us that small ships sometimes came to this river to trade with her people for skins and tortoise-shell; but none had been there for several months.

At first I thought that our wreck was entirely deserted, but after a time Uncle Naboth's pudgy form appeared at the stern, waving his red handkerchief in frantic greeting; a moment later our sailors flocked to his side, and then a lusty cheer of welcome saluted our grateful ears.

CHAPTER EIGHTEEN
THE PRINCESS DISAPPEARS

WE WERE GIVEN a joyful welcome by our comrades aboard the wreck, you may be sure. Ned was there, a smile mantling his rugged face as the auto came alongside and he assisted us to make fast and mount to the slanting deck of the ship.

Uncle Naboth's eyes were big and staring as our dainty Indian princess came aboard; but I could see that he was pleased with her beauty and modest demeanor.

No questions were asked us until we were all comfortably stowed on deck and the automobile had been hoisted over the side by the willing sailors and set in its old position. They were glad enough to see us safely returned without bothering us with questioning; but I knew of their eagerness to hear of our adventures and so took an early opportunity to remark:

"Well, Uncle Naboth and Ned, we've got the diamonds."

"Sure?"

"Sure enough."

I brought the basket and allowed them to inspect the treasure, which they did with wonder and a sort of awe, for they had little to say.

"How much is the bunch worth?" asked my uncle, trying to be indifferent.

"Why, we are all quite ignorant of their value," I replied; "but Moit and I both think we have secured a snug fortune for each one of us four who are interested in the division. We couldn't have done anything at all without the automobile, though, so I am going to give Duncan a part of my share."

"I won't take it," declared Moit. "We made a fair and square bargain, to share alike, and I mean to live up to it."

"But you need the money more than we do," I protested, "for you've got to build a factory to manufacture your machines and also to make a home for Ilalah. She is a prize we don't share in, but we'd like to contribute to her happiness, so I shall suggest to Ned and Uncle Naboth that you take a half of all the diamonds and we will divide the other half."

"Agreed!" cried my uncle and Ned, both together, and although Duncan objected in a rather pig-headed way I declared that we had fully made up our minds and he had nothing to say about the matter.

Then we told our story, rather briefly at first, for it would take some time to give our friends all the details of our adventures. Uncle was very proud of the way Bryonia and Nux had behaved, and told them so in his outspoken fashion. The honest fellows could have desired no higher reward.

After this Ned told me of his trip. On reaching the ocean he had rigged a mast and sail on the long boat and before a brisk breeze had soon reached Manzanillo Bay and arrived at Colon harbor within a half day.

Colon is a primitive town built upon a low coral island, but being the Atlantic terminal of the great canal it possessed an office of the Central and South American Telegraph Company, so that Ned was able to send a cable message by way of Galveston to Mr. Harlan.

He got an answer the next day, saying that the *Carmenia,* one of the Company's ships, was due at Cristobal in a few days, and further instructions as to the disposition of the wrecked cargo would be cabled me on her arrival. Cristobal was a port adjoining Colon, and I remembered to have heard that the *Carmenia* was soon to come home from the Pacific with a light cargo; so I judged it would be Mr. Harlan's intention to have her take our structural steel on board and carry it on to San Pedro.

All we could do now was to wait, and instead of waiting in unhealthy Colon, Ned wisely decided to return to the wreck and report to me.

They had begun to worry over us and to fear the Indians had murdered us, so it was a great relief to them when we came back safe and successful from our perilous adventure.

Uncle Naboth admired Ilalah more and more as he came to know her, and he told Duncan with great seriousness that she was worth more than all the diamonds in the world, to which absurd proposition the inventor gravely agreed. But indeed we were all fond of the charming girl and vied with one another to do her honor. Even stolid Ned Britton rowed across to the marshes in the afternoon and returned with a gorgeous boquet of wild flowers to place in the Indian maid's cabin—formerly his own cabin, but gladly resigned for her use.

Ilalah accepted all the attentions showered upon her with simple, unaffected delight, and confided to us that she had altered entirely her old judgment of the whites and now liked them very much.

"They must be my people, after this," she said, with a sad smile, "because I have left the Techlas forever."

At dinner Bryonia outdid himself as a chef and provided for the menu every delicacy the ship afforded. Ilalah ate little, but enjoyed the strange foods and unusual cooking. After dinner we sat on the deck in the splendid moonlight and recited at length our adventures, until the hour grew late.

When I went to bed I carried the diamonds to my locker, putting them carefully away where no one could get at

them until we left the wreck and the time came to make the division. The ship was very safe for the present. Until another severe gale occurred to bring the waves up the river there was no danger of her going to pieces, as she held firmly to her mud bank, weighted on her open planks with the great mass of steel in the hold. Her bottom was like a crate, but her upper works seemed as firm and substantial as ever.

Ilalah's cabin was on the starboard side, but in spite of the ship's listing her window was four or five feet above the surface of the river. She bade us a sweet good-night in her pretty broken English, and an hour later everyone on board was enjoying peaceful slumbers and I, for my part, was dreaming of the fortune we had so unexpectedly secured.

Suddenly a cry aroused me. I sat up and listened but could hear no further sound. Absolute silence reigned throughout the ship. Yet the cry still rang in my ears, and the recollection of it unnerved me.

While I hesitated a knock came to my door, and I got up and lighted a candle.

Moit was standing outside in the saloon. His face was white but as undecided in expression as my own.

"Did you hear anything, Sam?" he asked.

"Yes."

"Was it a cry for help?"

"That, or a woman's scream, Duncan."

"Come with me," he said, and I followed him to the door of Ilalah's cabin.

Two or three loud knockings failed to arouse any response. I turned the handle, found the door unlocked, and threw it open.

The room was empty.

I turned my flickering candle in every direction, lighting up the smallest cranny, as if the girl could be hidden in a rat-hole. The window stood wide open, and the cool night breeze came through it.

I turned toward Duncan, who stood in the middle of the room staring at the floor. As my gaze followed his, I saw several of the blue beads Ilalah had worn scattered over the carpet.

"It is Nalig-Nad," he muttered. "The San Blas have stolen my princess!"

"What's up, boys?" asked Uncle Naboth. He was standing in the doorway clad in a suit of pajamas that were striped like a convict's, only in more gorgeous colors.

"The Indians have stolen Ilalah and carried her away," I answered.

I am afraid Uncle Naboth swore. He is a mild mannered old gentleman, but having taken a strong liking for the beautiful girl he perhaps could find no other way, on the impulse of the moment, to express his feelings.

"Well," he remarked, after we had looked blankly into one another's faces for a time, "we must get her back again, that's all."

"Of course, sir," agreed Duncan, rousing himself. "We will go at once."

"What time is it?" I asked.

"Three o'clock," answered my uncle, promptly.

"Then let us wait until morning," I advised. "The Indians already have a good start of us and there would be no chance to overtake them before they regain the king's village. We must be cautious and lay our plans carefully if we hope to succeed."

"Perhaps you are right," returned Duncan, wearily. "But I swear to you, Sam, that I will find Ilalah and bring her back with me, or perish in the attempt."

I smiled at his theatric manner, but Uncle Naboth said seriously:

167

"I don't blame you a bit, sir. That girl is worth a heap o' trouble, and you can count on me to help you to the last gasp."

"Well, well," said I, impatiently, "let us get dressed and go on deck to talk it over." I well knew there would be no more sleep for us that night, and although I was not in love with the lost princess I was as eager to effect her rescue as Moit himself.

"But I must warn you, gentlemen," I continued, "that you have to deal with the wiliest and fiercest savage in existence, and if we venture into his dominions again the chances of our ever coming out alive are mighty slim."

"All right, Sam," retorted Uncle Naboth, cheerfully; "we've got to take those chances, my lad, so what's the use of grumbling?"

"If you're afraid, Sam—" began Moit, stiffly.

"Oh, get out!" was my peevish reply. "I may be afraid, and small wonder if I am; but you know very well I'll go with you. So get your togs on, both of you, and I'll meet you on deck."

CHAPTER NINETEEN
WE ATTEMPT A RESCUE

T HE ENTIRE SHIP'S company was aroused by this time, and it amused me to find that every man jack, down to the commonest sailor, was tremendously indignant and most properly incensed because Nalig-Nad had dared to steal his own daughter — the successor to his throne — from the white men with whom she had fled.

Ned Britton's plan was to arm our entire company "to the teeth" and march in solid ranks through the forest until we came to the king's village, which he figured lay about opposite the point where our ship had stranded. Once at the village we could surprise the place, capture Ilalah, and bear her in triumph back to the wreck.

There were several objections to Ned's optimistic plan. In the first place we did not know the forest, and the Indians did. They could hide behind the trees and pick us off with their arrows before we could use our fire-arms; or they might ambush us, and annihilate our band. Moreover, we were not sure Ilalah had been taken directly to the king's village. They might have hidden her somewhere else.

"It's another case of automobile, Mr. Moit," declared Uncle Naboth. "If we're a-goin' to get that girl you'll have to use the convertible, as sure as fate."

"There is no doubt of that," returned the inventor, promptly. "I have determined to start as soon as it is daylight."

"What is your idea, Duncan?" I asked.

"Simply to enter the country of the Techlas, show them a bold and fearless front, find out where the princess is, and then rescue her in some way. I'm afraid they will treat her badly, because she defied them and ran away with me."

"But she is to be their next ruler, after Nalig-Nad is dead," said I.

"Yes, if she outlives him. But the king has two other children, and he may prefer one of them to rule."

"That's a fact," I answered. "I've seen them. And Nalig-Nad must have been furious at Ilalah for favoring the hated whites."

"There is no time to lose," continued Duncan, nervously. "We must start as soon as possible and make our plans on the way. Who will go with me?"

Everyone wanted to go, of course; but finally it was settled that Uncle Naboth and I, with Nux and Bryonia, should accompany Duncan Moit in the automobile. If we did not return within twenty-four hours then Ned Britton was to land his sailors and march quickly through the forest to our rescue. This arrangement was the best we could think of, and when I frankly told the men that this hazardous duty would not be forced upon them, since the adventure was wholly outside their province as seamen, they one and all declared they would "see us through" or die in the attempt.

Only Dick Lombard, whose arm had been broken, and an old sailor with a bruised knee were to be left behind, that they might care for the ship in our absence.

"No one can steal the cargo, anyhow; it's too heavy," I remarked; "and if the Indians manage to do us up entirely Mr. Harlan will still be able to get his steel beams. So we need not worry over the ship."

It was a desperate enterprise, and we knew it; but so strong was our admiration for the Princess of the Techlas that we did not hesitate to attempt in her behalf all that brave men might be capable of.

At the first break of day we got the automobile over the side and safely launched it. There was not a moment's unnecessary delay, and as Duncan was now familiar with the river channel we were soon paddling at our best speed up the river.

By the time the red rays of the rising sun gleamed over the water we had passed the two hillocks and reached the southern tributary that led into the land of the Techlas.

We saw no Indians in the forest this time. Either it was too early for them to be abroad or they had assembled inland for some purpose. The forest was deserted.

Our progress was, of course, much slower than on land. I think the automobile paddled about eight miles an hour in still water, but as we now had to stem a current we made less time than that. But distances are not great in Panama, where the isthmus has a breadth of only some fifty miles, so that we were not long in passing the northern forest and coming to the coastal plains.

We left the river at the same spot as before, where the bank was low and shelving; for in talking over our plans we had decided to make directly for Nalig-Nad's own village. It was reasonable to suppose that Ilalah had been first taken there, it being the nearest point to the ship from whence they had stolen her. The king might intend to hide her, presently, even if he permitted his rebellious daughter to live; but we judged that he would not expect us to give chase so soon. That we would dare venture into his dominions a second time the astute monarch would hesitate to believe.

We relied much upon the promptness with which we had acted, and although we were forced to travel by a roundabout route we ought, with good luck, to reach the king's village by the middle of the forenoon.

Once on the broad and level plains Moit allowed his machine to do its best. We knew there were no obstruc-

171

tions in the way, so we made a wonderful dash across the country.

No effort was made by the San Blas to oppose us or interfere with our progress. We observed no warriors at all, and the few farmers we passed scarcely paused in their labors long enough to stare at us.

When we came to Ogo's village, however, we saw by means of the glass that the place was swarming with Indians, who were as busy and excited as bees in a hive. This puzzled us, and made us fear the princess might be in this place instead of the village farther on. But we decided to stick to our first programme, so we circled around the town to the north and continued on our way.

Much faster than we had covered the distance before, we now fled over the plain, and soon the enclosure became visible and our journey was almost over.

A great jagged section of the wall had been blown up by the explosion, wrecking some of the huts at the same time; but as we drew nearer we discovered that Nalig-Nad had caused a big ditch to be dug, in the form of a half moon, reaching from one end of the broken wall to the other. This ditch was evidently made on our account, and as it circled outward into the plain it prevented most effectually our entering the enclosure with the automobile.

We smiled at so childish an attempt to bar us from the village, but it informed us plainly that the king had anticipated our return and feared us, which knowledge served to encourage us very much.

We halted the machine outside the ditch, a hundred yards or so from the wall, and then proceeded to take careful observation of the condition of affairs at the village.

Our arrival had created no apparent excitement. There were no crowds to be seen and the few natives, men or women, who stalked across the space that was visible within the wall, going from one building to another, merely turned their faces toward us for a moment and then continued on their way. A woman sat at one side of the gap milking a goat; another near her was hanging some newly washed tunics on the edge of the broken wall to dry in the sun; but neither of these gave us more than a glance or allowed us to interrupt their occupation.

This apathy was mystifying. Surely we had created enough excitement at the time we left the king's village to ensure a degree of interest in our return. If the savages imagined their puny ditch any protection they were likely to find themselves much mistaken.

Presently we saw something that aroused us to action. Ilalah appeared, crossing the enclosure from one of the side huts to the king's palace. Her hands were bound firmly behind her back and her eyes were covered with a thick scarf which effectually blindfolded her. She was led and pushed along by two sour visaged old women, who showed their princess scant courtesy.

Moit swore roundly under his breath and I myself was filled with indignation at the poor girl's condition; at the same time we were gratified to know we had found her by coming promptly to the right place.

"Now," said Duncan, grimly, "we know what to do."

"What is it?" I enquired.

"They will bring her out again, sooner or later," he answered, "and then we must make a dash, seize her, regain the automobile, and fly back to the ship."

"Easy enough!" ejaculated Uncle Naboth, admiringly.

The women had finished milking and hanging out their clothes. Just now the courtyard seemed deserted.

"This is our chance," cried Moit. "Follow me, all of you except Mr. Perkins. He must stay to guard the machine and to wave us a signal when Ilalah appears. We will creep

173

up to the broken wall and hide behind it until the princess comes back. Then we will make a rush all together and capture her before the Indians know what we are about. Are you all armed?"

We were, and ready.

Duncan leaped from the car and we followed him. Then, bounding across the narrow ditch, we ran silently but quickly to a position behind the wall, where those inside could not see us. There we crouched, panting, to await Uncle Naboth's signal.

CHAPTER TWENTY
OUTWITTED

THE SILENCE OF death seemed to reign in the little village. All life had for the moment ceased, and gradually this extraordinary fact impressed me ominously.

"Where are all the people?" I whispered to Moit.

"I can't imagine," he answered.

"Guess dey in de co'te yard of de palace," said Bry, who with Nux stood just beside us. "Princess bein' judged; ev'body lookin' on."

That seemed plausible; and it was a condition especially favorable to our plans; so we waited with suppressed excitement, our eager eyes upon the automobile, until suddenly we saw Uncle Naboth spring to his feet and wave his red handkerchief.

At the signal we four rose as one man and dashed through the gap into the enclosure, each with a revolver held fast in either hand.

As I bounded over the loose rubbish something suddenly caught me and threw me violently to the ground, where I rolled over once or twice and then found myself flat upon my back with a gigantic Indian pressing his knee against my chest.

I heard a roar from Moit and answering shouts from our two blacks, and turning my head saw them struggling with a band of natives who surrounded them on every side.

Indeed, our conquest was effected much sooner than I can describe the event on paper, and within a few moments all four of us stood before our captors disarmed and securely bound.

I own I was greatly humiliated by the clever deception practiced upon us by Nalig-Nad. The wily king had foreseen our arrival and using Ilalah as a bait had ambushed us so neatly that we had no chance to fight or to resist our capture. The victory was his, and it was complete.

Stay; there was Uncle Naboth yet to be reckoned with. I could see him still standing in the car glaring with amazement at the scene enacted within the enclosure.

The Indians saw him, too, and with wild and triumphant yells a score of them rushed out and made for the car. But my uncle was warned and had calmly laid a number of revolvers upon the seat beside him.

With a weapon in either hand the old gentleman blazed away at the Techlas as soon as they approached, doing such deadly execution that the natives were thrown into confusion and held back, uncertain what to do.

Having emptied one brace of revolvers Mr. Perkins hurled them at the heads of his assailants and picked up another pair. I wondered that the San Blas did not shoot him down with arrows, or impale him on a spear, for the top was down and he was unprotected from such missiles; but doubtless they had been instructed to capture him alive and had not been prepared for such a vigorous resistance.

Presently an Indian who had made his way around to the opposite side put his hand on the rail and leaped lightly into the car; but my uncle turned in a flash and seized the fellow at the waist in his powerful arms. Lifting the astonished Techla high in the air Uncle Naboth flung him bodily into the furious crowd before him, tumbling a number of his foes to the ground with this living catapult.

But such magnificent strength and courage was without avail. Before uncle could seize his revolvers again a dozen warriors had leaped into the car beside him and grasped him so firmly that further struggles were useless. The little man collapsed immediately and was dragged out and brought to where we had been watching him in wonder and admiration.

"Good for you, Uncle!" I cried. "If we could have managed to put up such a fight it might have been a different story."

He smiled at us cheerily.

"Hain't had so much fun, my lads, since Polly had the measles," he panted; "but it couldn't last, o' course, 'cause I'm all out o' trainin'."

And now that all our party had been captured, transforming powerful enemies into helpless victims, King Nalig-Nad appeared before us with a calm countenance and ordered us taken to one of the huts, there to remain in confinement to await his pleasure concerning our disposal.

"Who's this feller?" asked Uncle Naboth, looking hard at the king.

"It is Nalig-Nad," I replied, rather depressed by our hard luck.

"Why, hello, Naddie, old boy — glad to meet you!" said Mr. Perkins, advancing as far as his captors would let him and holding out one of his broad, fat hands.

The king regarded him silently. It was the first time he had had an opportunity to inspect this addition to our former party. But he paid no attention to the outstretched hand.

"Know your daughter well," continued Uncle Naboth, unabashed at the marked coolness with which his friendly advances were met; "she's a fine gal, Nalig; oughter be proud o' her, old chap!"

With this he began to chuckle and poked the king jovially in his royal ribs, causing the stern visaged monarch to jump backward with a cry of mingled indignation and rage. This so pleased my uncle that his chuckle increased to a cough, which set him choking until he was purple in the face.

The king watched this exhibition with amazement, but when his prisoner recovered with startling abruptness and wiped the tears of merriment from his eyes, the barbarian gave a disdainful grunt and walked away to his palace. He was followed by his band of attendant chiefs, whom I recognized as his former counsellors.

I looked around for Ilalah, but she had disappeared the moment we rushed into the enclosure, having doubtless been dragged away by her attendants as soon as she had served the purpose of luring us into the trap.

We were now taken to one of the huts built against the wall and thrust through a doorway with scant ceremony. It was merely a one-roomed affair with thick walls and no furniture but a clay bench at the back. The only aperture was the doorway. Several stout warriors, well armed and alert, ranged themselves before this opening as a guard.

We were not bound, for having lost all our weapons, including even our pocket-knives, we were considered very helpless.

"I don't like the looks of this thing," I remarked, when we had seated ourselves quite soberly in a row on the mud bench.

"Bad box, sure 'nough, Mars' Sam," said Bryonia, with a sigh.

"I hope they won't touch the machine," observed Moit, nervously. "I don't mind what they do to me if they let the automobile alone."

"That's rubbish," said I in a petulant tone; "they couldn't run it to save their necks. Don't worry, old man."

"I s'pose we won't have much use for an auto-merbeel in the course of a jiffy or two," added my uncle, cheerfully.

178

"Oh, I depend a good deal upon Ned and his men," I replied. "He will be sure to come to our rescue early to-morrow morning."

"Too late, den, Mars' Sam," muttered Nux. "Dat wicked king ain't goin' let us lib long, I 'spect."

"Then why did he put us here?" I demanded. "If he intended to kill us quickly he'd have murdered us on the spot."

"There was nothing to prevent his doing that, most certainly," said Moit, eagerly adopting the suggestion.

This aspect of the affair was really encouraging. So elastic is hope in the breasts of doomed men that we poor creatures sat there for an hour or more and tried to comfort ourselves with the thought that a chance for escape might yet arise. It was pitiful, now that I look back upon it; but at the moment the outlook did not appear to us especially gloomy.

I do not believe that any regret for having followed the Indian girl and tried to rescue her entered into the mind of any one of the party. Ilalah had stood by us and it was our duty to stand by her, even had not Moit been so infatuated by her beauty that he could not be contented without her.

Being a boy and less stolid than my elders, I caught myself wondering if I should ever behold the handsome ship my father was building, and sighed at the thought that I might never stand upon its deck after all the ambitious plans we had laid for the future. There was a little comfort in the thought that all the diamonds were safe in the locker of the wreck and that Ned would look after them and carry my share as well as Uncle Naboth's to my father. But we were likely to pay a good price for the treasure we had wrested from the San Blas.

Midday arrived and passed. Food was brought to our guard but none was given to us. We were not especially

179

hungry, but this neglect was ominous. It meant that we had either not long to live or our foes intended to starve us. We tried to believe that the latter was the correct solution of the problem.

Soon after noon, however, all uncertainty vanished. Our guards entered, commanded by one of the chiefs, and said we were to be taken to judgment. They prepared us for the ordeal by tying our hands behind our backs with thongs, so securely that there was no way to slip the bonds. Then they fastened us together in a string by an original method.

A coil of dressed skin was brought and an Indian held one end while another made a slip-noose and threw it over Duncan's head. A second slip-noose was placed around Bryonia's neck, a third around that of Uncle Naboth, a fourth around Nux and the fifth around my own neck. There was still enough of the coil remaining for a second guard to hold — and there we were. If any one of us attempted to run, or even to struggle, he would only tighten his noose, and perhaps those of the others, and risk a choking.

It wasn't a bad method of keeping us orderly and meek, and we were not at all pleased with the arrangement, I assure you.

When we had been thus secured, the chief — who, by the way, was a "green chief" — ordered us sternly to march; and so, like a gang of chained convicts, we tramped from the gloomy hut and passed out into the courtyard.

CHAPTER TWENTY-ONE
THE SACRIFICE

THE ELABORATE PREPARATIONS made for our "judgment" were certainly flattering; but we were in no mood to appreciate the mocking attentions of the San Blas.

The open space of the enclosure in front of the palace was filled with a crowd of silent Indians, so many being present that we knew they must have gathered from all parts of the territory.

Our guards led us through the close ranks of these spectators to a clear place near the center, where King Nalig-Nad sat upon a bench with a score of his favorite green chiefs ranged just behind him. At the sides of this interesting group several women, all of whom had green in their tunics, squatted upon the ground. At the king's feet were the same pretty boy and girl I had seen on my first presentation to the potentate.

But this was not all. In the open space at the right of the king stood Ilalah between two stout guards. The girl's hands were bound behind her back as ours were, but she was no longer blindfolded. Her proud and beautiful face wore a smile as we were ranged opposite her, and she called aloud in English in a clear voice:

"Have fortitude, my White Chief. In death as in life Ilalah is your own."

A murmur of reproach came from those of the San Blas who understood her speech. The king looked at his daughter with a dark frown mantling his expressive features.

"And I belong to Ilalah," replied Duncan Moit, composedly, as he smiled back at his sweetheart.

181

Indeed, I was proud of the courage of all my comrades on this trying occasion. Bryonia and Nux were dignified and seemingly indifferent, Uncle Naboth smiling and interested in each phase of the dramatic scene, and the inventor as cool in appearance as if this gathering of the nation was intended to do him honor. I do not know how I myself bore the ordeal, but I remember that my heart beat so fast and loud that I was greatly annoyed for fear someone would discover its rebellious action and think me afraid. Perhaps I really was afraid; but I was greatly excited, too, for it occurred to me that I was facing the sunshine and breathing the soft southern air for almost the last time in my life. I was sorry for myself because I was so young and had so much to live for.

Ilalah, it seemed, was to be judged first because her rank was higher than that of the strangers.

The king himself accused her, and when he began to speak, his voice was composed and his tones low and argumentative. But as he proceeded his speech grew passionate and fierce, though he tried to impress upon his people the idea that it was his duty that obliged him to condemn Ilalah to punishment. However that plea might impress the Techlas it did not deceive us in the least. It was father against daughter, but perhaps the king's hatred of the whites had turned him against his first born, or else he preferred that the pretty girl nestling at his feet should succeed him.

"Lords and chiefs of the Techlas," he said, speaking in his native language, "the Princess Ilalah has broken our laws and outraged the traditions that have been respected in our nation for centuries. We have always hated the white race, and with justice. We have forbidden them to enter our dominions and refused to show them mercy if they fell into our hands. But this girl, whose birth and station are so high that she is entitled to succeed me as ruler of the Techlas, has violated our most sacred sentiments. She has favored and protected a band of white invaders; she has dared to love their chief, who has lied to us and tricked us; she has even forgotten her maidenly dignity and run away with him, preferring him to her own people. It is the law that I, her father, cannot judge or condemn her, although it is my privilege to condemn all others. Therefore I place her fate in the hands of my noble chiefs. Tell me, what shall be the fate of the false Techla? What shall be Ilalah's punishment?"

The chiefs seemed undecided and half frightened at the responsibility thus thrust upon them. They turned and consulted one another in whispers, casting uncertain looks at the princess, who smiled back at them without a trace of fear upon her sweet face.

Standing close beside Ilalah I now discovered our old friend Tcharn, the goldsmith and arrow-maker, whose eager face showed his emotion at the peril of his friend. His dark eyes roved anxiously from the girl to her judges, and it was plain to see that he was fearful of her condemnation.

I myself tried to read the decision of the chiefs from their faces, and decided that while Ilalah was doubtless a great favorite with them all, they could find no excuse for her conduct. Their conference lasted so long that the king grew impatient, and his animosity became more and more apparent as he glowered menacingly upon the girl and then glanced appealingly at her judges, who tried to avoid his eyes.

Finally, however, the conference came to an end.

A tall, lean chief, whose gray hairs and the prominence of the green stripes in his tunic evidently entitled him to be the spokesman, stepped forward and bowed low before the king.

"Mighty Ruler of the Techlas," he said, "we have weighed well the strange conduct of the Princess Ilalah and desire to ask her a question."

"The speech of the accused may not be considered," said the king, gruffly.

"It affects not her condemnation, but rather her punishment," returned the other.

"Then proceed."

"Princess," continued the old man, speaking in a kindly tone as he addressed the young girl, "if in our mercy we spare your life will you promise to forsake your white chief and yield him and his followers to our vengeance?"

"No!" she answered, proudly.

Her questioner sighed and turned to his fellows, who nodded to him gravely.

"Then," said he, again turning to the king, "we find that the conduct of the Princess Ilalah merits punishment, and the punishment is death!" The king smiled triumphantly and cast a look around the assemblage. Not a man or woman returned his smile. They stood steadfast as rocks, and only the little arrow-maker gave way to his grief by bowing his head in his hands and sobbing most pitifully.

"We also find," continued the grave chieftain, breaking the painful pause, "that the law forbids any Techla to lift a hand against one of the royal blood; and especially is that person immune who is next in succession to the throne." This statement caused a thrill that could not be repressed to pass through the crowd. The natives looked on one another curiously, but satisfaction lurked in their dark eyes.

I began to like these people. In themselves they were not especially disposed to evil, but their fiendish king had dictated their thoughts and actions for so long that they were virtually the slaves of his whims.

"HE DREW THE BOWSTRING TO HIS CHIN."

"Therefore," said the chief, speaking in a firm voice, "who will execute our decree of death upon the royal princess?"

"I will!" cried Nalig-Nad, springing to his feet. "The king is bound by no law save his own will. The girl is condemned to death, and die she shall!"

With a lightning gesture he caught up his bow and notched an arrow.

I looked toward Ilalah. Her face was palid and set but she did not flinch for an instant. One fleeting glance she gave into Duncan's face and then turned her eyes steadily upon her fierce and enraged sire.

The king did not hesitate. He drew the bowstring to his chin, took rapid aim, and loosed the deadly shaft.

A cry burst from the assemblage, and even while it rang in my ears I saw Tcharn leap into the air before the princess, receive the arrow in his own breast, and then fall writhing in agony upon the ground.

CHAPTER TWENTY-TWO
THE THRUST OF A SPEAR

INSTANTLY THERE WAS tumult all about us. The crowd broke and surged toward the central point in the tragedy, forcing us who were in front to struggle on the crest of the wave. Their reserve vanished and each man cried to his neighbor in eager tones and allowed the mad excitement of the moment full sway.

Someone cut Ilalah's bonds and the girl sank to the ground to support the head of the little arrow-maker upon her breast, pressing back his thin locks and tenderly kissing him upon the forehead.

But he knew nothing of this grateful kindness. His eyes were set and glazed, for the arrow had lodged in his heart.

A tug at my thong threatened to strangle me, for Moit had bounded forward to kneel beside Ilalah and try to assist her in spite of his own helpless condition. Then some semblance of order was restored and our guards pushed us back and eased the thong which was fast throttling me.

From the murmured words of the natives I gathered that Tcharn had atoned by his sacrifice for all the guilt charged against the princess, as the law declared that when the death penalty was imposed another could die instead of the condemned and so set him free.

For this reason the king was raging like a wild beast and threatening those who expressed sympathy for the girl who had so miraculously escaped his brutal vengeance.

"But the whites, at least, shall die—and the black men who are with them!" he shouted aloud, casting at us such glances of hatred and ferocity that we knew our fate was sealed.

They had carried poor Tcharn away and the princess had risen to her feet and now stood bravely confronting her father.

"It is folly to talk of injuring these strangers," she answered him, boldly. "I alone know their wonderful powers and that they are able to crush us all if we dare attempt to harm them."

The king let out a disdainful roar, but Ilalah's words impressed many in the crowd and caused the Techlas to murmur again.

"What can they do?" asked Nalig-Nad, derisively. "They are but human and they are in our power."

"They have their magic chariot," she said, "which you all know can deal death and destruction to their foes."

"Magic!" retorted the king, laughing boisterously; "do you call that poor, man-made contrivance magic?"

All eyes turned toward the opening, where a hundred yards beyond the broken wall poor Moit's automobile was standing motionless as we had left it.

Most of those present had witnessed the machine's marvelous performances, and in nearly every face now lurked an expression of awe or apprehension. Nalig-Nad saw the look, and it aroused him to fury.

"Come!" he cried, "I will prove that the white men have no magic."

Seizing a heavy, bronze-tipped spear from an attendant he ran from the enclosure and made directly for the automobile, followed by a crowd of his most devoted adherents. The others, with us, remained to watch curiously what he would do.

I saw Moit's face pale and his lips tremble; but he stood firm and steadfast while the king rushed upon his beloved machine and with a powerful stroke drove the spear clean through the plates of sheathing which protected the body.

I own I was amazed at such a display of strength, but a more athletic savage than Nalig-Nad I have never beheld. When the jagged rent was torn in the side of the automobile the crowd that surrounded it danced gleefully and jeered at the helpless child of our poor inventor's brain as if it were alive and could feel their scorn.

Again Nalig-Nad seized a spear and hurled it at the side of the machine, piercing once more the light but stout metal. A third went crashing into the automobile, and then—

And then it seemed as though the world had suddenly come to an end.

I was dashed so forcibly against the huge body of my guard that where he fell upon the hard earth his head was crushed in like an eggshell. But I did not know this until I came to my senses and heard the sounds of moaning all around me and saw the ground covered with the forms of the stricken natives.

A knife severed my bonds and set me free, and I staggered to my feet to find Ilalah and Duncan Moit supporting me until I could recover sufficiently to stand alone.

Nux and Bryonia, all unhurt, were busy restoring the bruised and bewildered Techlas to consciousness, while Uncle Naboth sat upon the king's bench, his clothing torn to tatters, and wiped away with his red handkerchief the blood that trickled from a cut in his head.

I looked around wonderingly, trying to imagine what had happened, and saw a piece of dull silver metal driven edgewise into the front of the palace, where it was wedged firmly into the hard clay. That gave me a hint, and I looked out upon the plain where the automobile had stood and found that it had disappeared. So had Nalig-Nad and the crowd of furious natives that had surrounded him as he plunged his spear into the heart of Duncan Moit's great invention.

Then I remembered the can of glycerine explosive and knew the whole terrible story in an instant. The spear-point had made Ilalah Queen of the Techlas. It had also deprived her lover of the perfect fruit of years of inspired thought and faithful toil.

CHAPTER TWENTY-THREE
THE DESERTER

WHILE THE VILLAGE slowly recovered from the effects of this dreadful calamity and the uninjured were caring for their less fortunate brethren, our party was ushered into a comfortable apartment of the palace and given food and drink and such comforts as the place afforded.

We saw nothing of Ilalah at the time, for with those chiefs left to her she was doing her best to relieve the misery of the stricken village. Moit was with her, alert and active, keeping constantly by her side and eagerly assisting her in the work of mercy. This I learned afterward. Just then I imagined him frantic with grief and despair, and I found myself regretting the destruction of his great invention even more than the loss of life caused by the explosive. The dead were unimportant savages; the machine that had perished with them was the most splendid achievement, I firmly believe, that any man in any era of civilization has ever been able to boast.

But when toward evening Duncan Moit came to us with Ilalah, I was astonished at his placid stoicism. Grieved he certainly was, but his face expressed resolve and thoughtfulness more than despair.

"I'm awfully sorry, old man," I said, laying a sympathetic hand upon his shoulder. "I know how long and tedious the time will seem until you are able to construct another machine as perfect as the one you have lost."

He shuddered a little at my words but replied gently:

"Sam, I shall never build another machine. That dream is over."

"Over!" I cried, astonished. "What do you mean? Will you abandon all your ambitions — the certain fortune that awaits you — the applause and admiration of your fellow men?"

"What do they all amount to?" he asked. "Yes; I abandon them. I'm going to live with Ilalah."

"Here?"

"Here; in the half savage and almost unknown land of the Techlas. The result of years of labor has been wiped out of existence in a flash, and I have not the courage to begin all over again. I have no patterns of the machine and the drawings and specifications all were destroyed with it. I could never build another that would equal it in perfection. But why should I attempt it? I do not need an automobile here. I do not need fortune, or fame, or anything but love; and this Ilalah has given me freely."

"Do I understand you to mean that you will always remain in this forsaken country?"

"That is my intention," he said. "I shall help my wife to rule her people and in her companionship be happy in a simple, natural way."

We argued with him long and earnestly, while Ilalah sat beside him silent and smiling but very sure that we could not prevail over his sudden but preposterous resolution.

They found a few scraps of what they believed to have once been Nalig-Nad, and that night the remains were consumed with fire, accompanied by many impressive ceremonies. Other funeral pyres burned also, both in the enclosure and on the plain beyond; for the most malignant of the green chiefs had followed the king to assist him in destroying the automobile and had therefore shared his fate.

Bright and early next morning Ned Britton appeared at the edge of the forest leading his band of seamen to our rescue. We advanced eagerly to meet him and told him the news of the king's destruction and of our altered standing with the new ruler of the San Blas. Ned had heard and felt the explosion even on the wreck, but thought that it must have been an earthquake.

The newcomers were not regarded with much favor by the Indians, yet I thought that we all assisted greatly to lend dignity to the day's ceremonies, which included the formal acknowledgment of Ilalah as ruler and lawgiver of the nation and her subsequent marriage—a most primitive rite—to the inventor, Duncan Moit. Ilalah's husband was next adopted as a Techla, and then the excitement seemed to subside and the population settled down to business again.

However, there was no denying the fact that the natives resented our presence among them and were ill at ease while we remained in the village. So I told "King Duncan," as Uncle Naboth insisted upon jocosely calling him, that we would make haste to return to our ship.

He offered no objection to our going, but stated simply that it would be our wisest course. Then he hesitated a moment, as if embarrassed, and added:

"You must never come back, you know. The Techlas will live their own lives in their own way, and hereafter I am to be one of them and shall forget everything that exists outside our borders. We permit you to go freely now, as a return for your kindness to our queen; but should you be daring enough to return at any time I warn you that you will be received as enemies, and opposed to the death."

"Will you become another Nalig-Nad, then?" I asked, indignant at the traitorous words.

"In the future, as in the past, the demoralizing influences of the whites and their false civilization will be excluded from the dominions of the San Blas," he answered, coolly. "My wife will rule as her fathers did, in spite of the fact that one white man has been admitted into the community. You have been my friends, but when you leave me now you must forget our friendship, as I am resolved to do. Should you invade the country of the Techlas again, you do so at your peril."

This assertion, coming from one whom I had trusted and regarded as a faithful comrade, filled me with consternation not unmixed with resentment. But the man had always been peculiar and I tried to make allowances for his erratic nature.

"Tell me, then," I said, after a moment's thought; "how about dividing those diamonds?"

"They are yours. I have no use for such things now," he added, a touch of sadness in his voice. "You are welcome to whatever share was due me — on one condition."

"What is that, Duncan?"

"That you will tell no one where you found them and will promise never to return here for more."

I hesitated, and Uncle Naboth looked sorely disappointed.

"It is my intention," continued Moit, firmly, "to support the traditions of the Techlas. They must own nothing that will arouse the cupidity of the outside world, for only in this way will they be able to control their own territory. I am glad the audacious Tcharn is dead, and I will destroy all his pretty goldsmith work within the next few days. Also I shall have the valley of diamonds thoroughly searched and all the white pebbles cast into the sea. Therefore no temptation will exist for you or your fellows to come here again. Our laws will be rigidly maintained, and any strangers, white or black, who defy them will be severely punished."

Yes, I had always suspected a streak of madness in Moit. Perhaps the destruction of his marvelous invention had served to unbalance a mind already insecurely seated. Anyway, I could see that he was in deadly earnest and that any argument would be useless. My companions, also, noted a strange glitter in his eyes that warned them he would not lift a finger to save their lives if they again ventured to invade the country ruled by Queen Ilalah.

So, with regret, we submitted to the inevitable. We bade Duncan Moit and his beautiful bride farewell and marched away through the forest till we came to the banks of the river, where the wreck lay in plain sight. A strong escort of silent natives watched us until we were all on board, and then they melted away and disappeared like ghosts.

I have never seen the inventor since, or stepped a foot upon the land of the Techlas.

CHAPTER TWENTY-FOUR
WE LEAVE PANAMA

WELL, THE STORY is told, as you may easily guess. Uncle Naboth and I ran up to Colon, and not liking that city took a train across the isthmus to Panama, which we liked no better. The people we met were a miserable lot, and did not compare either in intelligence or dignity with the isolated tribes of the San Blas. Some day, however, when the great canal is built, Americans will invade these parts in such numbers that the present population will disappear.

It is a mistake to think the climate of Panama unhealthful. On the uplands, both north and south of the depression where the canal zone is established, it is as healthful as any tropical country in the world. In the zone itself, which is ten miles wide, bad sanitation caused by the carelessness of the French workmen used constantly to breed fevers and disease. The Americans are now busily cleansing the Augean stables and good sanitary conditions are rapidly being established. But I will say this: that unless one has business in Panama he may readily discover a more desirable location for a residence.

We soon returned to the wreck, which we preferred to the towns of the isthmus, and there amused ourselves until the *Carmenia* arrived at Colon. Then her captain, an active and energetic young man named Colton, took charge of the remains of the *Gladys H.* He had received orders to remove the cargo, strip the wreck of all valuables and then abandon her where she lay.

He brought his ship alongside with ease and as soon as he was in charge and had given me a receipt, our people removed their personal possessions and were rowed round to Colon, where a steamer was shortly due that would carry us to New Orleans.

I kept an eye upon the forest for Moit, thinking he might appear to bid us good-bye; but he did not. We warned Captain Colton not to land in the San Blas country, but did not confide to him any part of our recent remarkable experiences.

A few days later we caught the steamer and made a quick voyage across the gulf. We reached Chelsea on the twelfth day of February, and were warmly welcomed by my father, who reported the *Seagull* nearing completion.

The diamonds were sold for a surprising amount of money, because the stones proved exceptionally large and perfect, and the proceeds were equally divided between Ned Britton, Uncle Naboth and myself. We had selected three good specimens of the "white pebbles" to sell for the benefit of our faithful seamen, and the amount of prize money they received from this source greatly delighted them. Nux and Bryonia would never accept anything in the way of money at all. They said that they belonged to Uncle Naboth and "Mars Sam," and they knew very well that whatever we had they were welcome to.

Neither Mr. Harlan nor his company ever blamed me for the loss of the *Gladys H.* It was one of those fateful occurrences that mortal man is powerless to control.

Sam Steele's Adventures

The Amazing Bubble Car

This text of this book is set in 10 point Book Antiqua.
The running titles & other decorative type
are set in Copperplate Gothic Bold.
The text and cover have been
designed by David Maxine
at Hungry Tiger Press
in San Diego.

This book was originally published in
1907 by the Reilly & Britton Company
of Chicago under the title
SAM STEELE'S ADVENTURES IN PANAMA.

THE PAWPRINT ADVENTURES

The Complete "Young Adult" Novels of L. Frank Baum

Sam Steele, the Daring Twins, the Flying Girl, Mary Louise, and Aunt Jane's Nieces all await you in this much-anticipated publishing project. Over two dozen volumes in all—this new series will be the most significant contribution to L. Frank Baum's legacy in decades!

Each classic volume is presented in a handsome new edition— beautifully repackaged in a *matching* hardcover format with their original illustrations. Don't miss a single title!

Hungry Tiger Press
5995 Dandridge Lane, Suite 121, San Diego, CA 92115-6575
w w w . h u n g r y t i g e r p r e s s . c o m

CPSIA information can be obtained at www.ICGtesting.com
Printed in the USA
BVOW03*1619040314

346274BV00002B/9/P

9 781929 527236